Praise for Beth Williamson's
Devils on Horseback: Gideon

"The adventure, the romance, it has it all. The love scenes were sensually romantic and they will curl your toes. This is the kind of story that will have you longing for a big, handsome cowboy of your own to come meandering into your backyard."

~ *Love Romances & More*

"Lovers of Beth Williamson's stories will like this book and those who enjoy American historical romances will find this a first-rate addition to their libraries…You can't find one any better than this."

~ *Dr. J's Book Place*

"I have never read a Beth Williamson novel I didn't like. This series is some of her very best work."

~ *The Romance Studio*

"…another exceptional addition to the Devils on Horseback series."

~ *Romance Junkies Reviews*

Beth Williamson delivers a healthy dose of action, suspense, drama and love in *Devils on Horseback: Gideon*."

~ *Literary Nymphs Reviews*

Look for these titles by
Beth Williamson

Now Available:

Marielle's Marshal
Branded
Hell for Leather
Secret Thoughts: Erotique
Secret Thoughts: Lustful

The Malloy Family Series
The Bounty
The Prize
The Reward
The Treasure
The Gift
The Tribute
The Legacy

Private Lives
On His Knees

The Devils on Horseback Series
Nate
Jake
Zeke
Lee
Gideon

Print Anthologies
Midsummer Night's Steam: Sand, Sun and Sex
Leather and Lace
Secret Thoughts

Devils on Horseback: Gideon

Beth Williamson

Samhain Publishing, Ltd.
11821 Mason Montgomery Road, 4B
Cincinnati, OH 45249
www.samhainpublishing.com

Devils on Horseback: Gideon
Copyright © 2012 by Beth Williamson
Print ISBN: 978-1-60928-437-4
Digital ISBN: 978-1-60928-429-9

Editing by Sasha Knight
Cover by Scott Carpenter

This book is a work of fiction. The names, characters, places, and incidents are products of the writer's imagination or have been used fictitiously and are not to be construed as real. Any resemblance to persons, living or dead, actual events, locale or organizations is entirely coincidental.

All Rights Are Reserved. No part of this book may be used or reproduced in any manner whatsoever without written permission, except in the case of brief quotations embodied in critical articles and reviews.

First Samhain Publishing, Ltd. electronic publication: April 2011
First Samhain Publishing, Ltd. print publication: March 2012

Dedication

To the memory of my friend Donna F, who passed away in August 2009. She was the epitome of strength, grace and courage. A woman who fought the fight for five long years and left behind a legacy of love. She taught me how to be brave even in the face of a mortal enemy. We miss you.

Chapter One

May 1868

"Who the hell are you?"

Gideon Blackwood stopped in his tracks, a puff of dust kicking up from his boots. He kept his arms at his sides, his breathing even, although his heart thundered like a horse's hooves. From the gruff, raspy quality of the voice behind him, he didn't know who he was dealing with.

"My name is Gideon Blackwood."

"What do you think you're doing sneaking around my wagon, Gideon Blackwood?"

Ah, it was definitely a woman. Whoever she was, she'd be no match for a man of his size, no matter how angry she sounded. As a veteran of the Civil War and countless battles, midnight raids and numerous wounds, not much scared him.

He turned around slowly so as not to spook her. To his surprise, he found a short figure wearing a dress that could've been used to hold potatoes and a floppy, ugly-as-hell wide hat that completely hid her face. The one thing that kept his attention was the pistol in her hand. That hand wasn't shaking either. He took stock of his opponent in the blink of an eye. She was barely over five feet tall, her shape hidden by the sack she wore. Gideon took a step toward her, and she cocked the gun.

"Answer the question." Her tone was as cold as the metal of the barrel.

Gideon couldn't judge her age since her face was covered and her voice deep for a female. She could be twelve or ninety, which meant he couldn't estimate how fast she'd be if he decided to disarm her.

Damn.

"I was riding to Grayton to see a friend of mine. I saw the busted wheel on the wagon and thought I could help." He never expected his attempt would result in having a woman hold a gun on him.

"Hero, eh? You a Johnny Reb?"

Gideon clenched his fists as he told himself to ignore the caustic nickname. He'd fought in the war for what he thought was right, same as every other man. It had been three years since the war ended, and she had no call to insult him. He had to keep his control, no matter what flew out of her mouth.

"We're all just folks now, ma'am. I'm no hero, and I sure don't want to be shot for trying to help out other folks in need. I'll be on my way." Gideon took a step away from the wagon. The stupid gelding placidly munched on grass while his master had a gun pointed at him.

"Hold it, mister. I didn't give you leave to walk away." She took a step sideways, and her boots crunched on the dirt.

"I don't need your permission, lady. Now either shoot me or let me go, because I'm done standing here jawin' with you." This time he did walk toward his horse.

"Wait, uh, please." The words seemed torn from her throat. "We do need help." She sighed so hard he'd swear the grass moved from the force of it.

He almost kept walking. Almost. But the Southern

gentleman inside him protested loudly. A woman asking for help was never ignored, no matter how ornery she was. Gideon sometimes cursed his sense of honor; it could be a pain in the ass.

Perhaps it was his own stress making him short-tempered. He'd left Tanger behind, along with all the pressures from his friends and family. If one more person had shoved a sister or daughter at him, proclaiming Gideon the most eligible bachelor in town, he'd have punched someone. Then his cousin Zeke, as sheriff, would have had to put his ass in jail. Instead Gideon had left town, or escaped was more like it. He had been headed to their friend Nate's ranch over in Grayton, several days' ride from Tanger if he was riding alone and unhindered.

Now, of course, it would take him much longer, considering he had stopped to help someone. Or rather been held at gunpoint when he tried to help. Gideon needed to relax, to get away from the loco idea he required a wife. Just because his cousins Zeke and Lee and his half brother Jake had found marital bliss, didn't mean Gideon had to. Although Nate was also happily married, his wife Eliza was a trouser-wearing straight shooter who would likely never try to force a female on anyone.

He needed to get to Grayton.

Gideon turned back toward her, hands on hips. "What do you need help with?" Too bad he sounded as gracious as she did, which was not at all.

"The wheel broke."

"I can see that."

She snorted. "I ain't big enough to get the wagon up on my own, and Granny can't get the new wheel on. We've been stuck here for a few days now."

"There are two of you?" He glanced around but didn't see

another soul.

"Four, actually. The twins are in the wagon with Granny." She gestured to the canvas that appeared to have strange-looking cargo beneath it.

"Twins?" Gideon hoped like hell it wasn't babies. Not that he didn't like young'uns, but he sure didn't want to have to rescue a young woman, two babies and an old woman. Jesus, what the hell had he stumbled into?

"The branch I found to leverage up the wagon broke. If we can find a sturdier one, I can change out the wheel."

Gideon eyeballed her. "Ma'am, you're no bigger than a minute and likely no older than one either. I don't think you could even get the wheel off, much less get a new one on."

She yanked off the hat, and a mass of curls popped out in a color explosion worthy of a sunrise. The woman glared at him, and he realized his mistake in a heartbeat—she was at least twenty, if not older. And she had a temper to match that hair.

"I've managed to get us from Virginia to Texas, driving the wagon and keeping everyone else healthy and fed. All I need from you is half an hour to change out the wheel." She threw her arms wide. "If'n you don't want to help, then be on your way."

"I told you I'd help, but I think we need more than just me."

She snorted. "Then you ain't no kind of Southern man I know. Be on your way, then." The woman had the audacity to turn her back on him.

Gideon didn't know whether to laugh or be insulted. This little bird had a lot of gumption, that was for sure.

"I didn't say I couldn't do it. I said I didn't think you could." He crossed his arms over his chest and widened his stance.

A breath hissed through her teeth. "You want to repeat

that?"

"Not particularly. Do you want my help or not?" He looked around and spotted a likely branch on the side of the road. He'd also need a fulcrum, something to use to leverage up the wagon.

"Quit your foolishness, Chloe. The man is offering to help." An even tinier figure emerged from behind the wagon. Her silver hair marked her as the granny, and her poke bonnet marked her as a woman who was from another era. She peered at Gideon. "And he's big enough to get the job done."

Chloe. A biblical name. How ironic was that? He and the Devils had biblical names—a fact that had made them hoot with laughter when they'd sat around darkened woods waiting for orders during the war. Now this woman had come into his life and she was saddled with a biblical name too. Fate surely was fickle.

"Thank you, ma'am." He nodded to the older woman. "Gideon Blackwood."

"I heard you the first time. I'm Henrietta Ruskin, and this here's my granddaughter, Chloe." She stood beside the younger woman, and he could hardly believe there was a six-inch height difference between them. Had he stumbled upon a group of tiny people with bad manners?

"Pleasure to meet you both, ma'am."

Not really.

"I'll get to work, then." Gideon headed for the branch, ignoring the furious whispering of the women behind him. Something about Chloe made him want to get on his horse and ride as fast as he could out of there. Now that he was committed to helping the Ruskin family, he couldn't leave just yet.

Damn.

Chloe was hopping mad. She didn't want help, and sure didn't want a stranger's help. He was big, which meant he could just take what he wanted and leave her and her family there. It frustrated her to feel this way, and it pricked her pride to ask for a stranger's assistance.

Granny made it worse by chastising her like Chloe was a young'un with her hand in the cookie jar. She was twenty years old, for God's sake. It had taken them months to get enough supplies together to leave Virginia, and she'd be damned if a broken wheel prevented them from reaching Corpus Christi. Granny's sister Julia lived there with her husband, or at least she had up until six months ago when her letters stopped coming.

Getting stranded on the side of the road for days was not what Chloe wanted to be doing. It fried her patience to have to wait for a big strong man to help her. Some days she hated being short.

"What's he doing?"

"I don't know. Looking for a sturdier branch, I would guess." Chloe stuffed her hat back on her head. "Jesus, Granny, did you have to take me to task like that?"

"Don't blaspheme."

"Pot calling the kettle black."

Granny narrowed her ice-blue eyes. "I've raised you since you was two years old and your mama died. Don't you sass me."

Truly her granny had been the only mother Chloe knew. She'd been tough but fair, teaching a young, motherless girl how to know wrong from right, to cook and sew, as well as how to fish and hunt. Her pa was as useless as teats on a boar when it came to most everything but spending money at the poker table. He'd used up every bit of luck he had five years earlier when he'd been caught cheating. Chloe had cried when they'd buried him. She had loved him, although he'd never been a father to her except when he had planted his seed.

Now she was stuck in some godforsaken spot in east Texas with a blue-eyed cowboy sporting an attitude as big as his shoulders. And that was mighty big.

"Sorry, Granny." Chloe blew out a breath. "I just want to be on our way. The stranger kind of riled me a bit."

"A bit?" Granny folded her arms over her chest.

Chloe scowled. "It doesn't matter anyway. He'll help us, and I won't have to see him again." She nodded toward the wagon. "What are the twins doing?"

"Napping. They ran around a lot this morning, and they just collapsed." Granny shook her head. "Two five-year-old girls is more trouble than one, that's for sure."

The last thing Granny and Chloe needed was two little girls to take care of. After the girls' mama died of heartbreak when her husband didn't come back from the war, the Ruskins took the girls in. Chloe learned firsthand how to be a mother, although some days she sure didn't want to. Hazel and Martha were good girls, even if they were a handful.

"Let's keep them in there, because that big cowboy didn't sound keen on the idea of little girls." Chloe started tucking her hair back under the hat.

"Little girls?" The stranger was back and this time with what seemed like an entire tree on his shoulder. The man was stronger than he looked, which she thought an impossible feat.

Chloe tried not to notice the size of the muscles clearly defined beneath the dark blue shirt the man wore, but holy hell, it was hard not to. She was only as tall as his shoulder, and with the tree up on top of it, he was larger than life. Her blood thumped through her veins, reverberating within her as though she was a plucked string.

Granny elbowed her. "Never you mind about little girls, Mr. Blackwood."

As he looked expectantly at Chloe, a shiver snaked down her spine although it was a warm, sunny day. She was no fool—she knew that people were like any other kind of animals and were attracted to each other. It had happened to her with a few boys back in Virginia, but there weren't many around when she was old enough to want to get hitched. Those who came back had too many ghosts in their eyes and too many troubles of their own.

If this stranger had ghosts, they were well hidden behind his annoyed expression. He scowled at her. "Ma'am?"

Oh Lord, she'd been staring at him. Chloe wanted to slap her forehead, but instead she scowled back at him. "That all you need?"

He gestured behind her. "No, I need that big rock right there too. It'll be easier if we use a fulcrum to leverage it up."

Chloe didn't know what a fulcrum was, but the rock was bigger than she and Granny put together. "How are you going to move that?"

"By rolling it."

"Oh. That makes sense." She peered at him. "What are you waiting for, then?"

"You are a prickly little thing, aren't you?" His brows drew even closer together. "I'm not standing here with this thing on my shoulder because I wanted splinters."

She swallowed the chuckle that threatened. "Then let's get to it."

He turned and walked to the wagon, setting the branch

down. Chloe moved to the rock and started digging to loosen the soil around it. She didn't get very far before he nudged her out of the way and yanked the damn thing out of the ground. Dirt clods flew every which way, sending her scrambling backward to wipe her eyes and face.

Chloe sputtered and wanted to tell him exactly what he could do with the rock instead of rolling it to the wagon. By the time she got all the muck out of her face and eyes, he had set the rock beneath the wagon and put the branch on it.

"What are you doing?"

"Testing the branch to be sure it's strong enough."

"You're going to lift up the wagon."

"Therein lies the way to take off the broken wheel."

"The girls are in the wagon. You'll scare them to death." Chloe got to her feet and glanced at Granny. "Let's get them out of there."

"They're in the wagon? I thought she said—"

"She said to never mind about them, but obviously now we'll need to." Chloe lifted the tarp and climbed into the wagon.

The girls were snuggled together under the yellow quilt they'd carried from their home. The white-blonde moppets were identical with their chocolate brown eyes and soft honey skin. They were full of mischief, sweetness, energy and intelligence. Despite the extra work of taking care of them, Chloe loved them like they were her little sisters.

She picked up Hazel and scuttled backward until she was out from under the tarp and handing the sleeping child to Granny. "Put her under the shade of that big cottonwood over there. I'll get Martha."

Sweat trickled down Chloe's temple as she crawled back in to retrieve the other child. Truly, she wasn't an angry person by nature, but too many years of hunger, heartache and desperation had turned her into one. The stranger had offered help, and she'd nearly bitten off his nose for it. Granny had been right about needing assistance, but Chloe hadn't wanted to accept it. There was too much pride on her narrow shoulders, her biggest flaw amongst a dozen or two.

Martha mumbled as Chloe made her way back outside and let herself down as slowly as she could. She glanced over at the stranger, and he looked positively horrified by the sight of the child in her arms. Chloe rolled her eyes and walked over to where Granny waited in the shade of the tree. She laid the girl down next to her sister and straightened, her back already screaming in protest after two days of trying to fix the wheel herself.

"He's waiting on you."

"I know he is." Chloe kept her voice as low as Granny's. "I just needed a minute to get the kinks out of my back."

"Uh-huh. You'd best get over there and get that wheel fixed." Granny raised one silver brow, a knowing look in her eyes.

Chloe huffed and went back to the wagon, her fists buried in her lower back to ease the knots. She came around the side, and much to her surprise, the stranger was staring at her chest. She glanced down and noted that her pitiful tits actually looked nice and round when she pushed them out like that.

Well, holy shit, wasn't that a first?

Her head snapped up, and she narrowed her eyes. "Something you want to say, mister?"

He appeared almost flustered as he averted his gaze and scowled at the wagon. "About time you got back here. I do have someplace to go, you know."

Chloe wanted to find out just what he thought of her, but

she didn't want to appear to be a floozy or worse, fishing for compliments. She knew she was no beauty, but perhaps there were parts of her that weren't too bad.

"There's a stump I brought over. I'm going to leverage the wagon up with the rock. You're going to have to roll the stump under there to support the weight of the wagon so we can change out the wheel." He pointed at a gnarly looking, moss-covered piece of wood. "You need to make sure you can move it."

Chloe hmphed and rolled the stump over to the wagon, realizing a bit too late that she'd showed Mr. Blackwood a full view of her hind end. She straightened up quickly and scowled at him.

"See, I can move it just fine. Let's get this done without any more talking." She didn't want to sound mean, but her temper was frayed beyond normal.

"That's exactly what I want to do." Mr. Blackwood picked up the log again, reminding Chloe how strong the man was.

He positioned it in the middle of the wagon while she was close to the broken wheel at the front. With a mighty grunt, he applied pressure, and the wagon moved about an inch upward. He heaved again, and this time all the veins stood out in his face and neck. The wagon moved perhaps an inch and a half.

"Son of a bitch." He breathed heavily as he wiped his brow with one shirt sleeve. "What the hell is in that wagon?"

Chloe turned to look. "What's in it? Our things." She was no fool, not about to tell this stranger exactly what they had. Who knew if he'd steal it and leave them really stranded? She had to be smarter than that.

"What kind of things?" He set the log down and stepped toward the canvas. "Please don't tell me there's furniture."

"Hey, don't touch that." Chloe grabbed his arm as he reached for the rope holding the canvas down.

"If you want help, then I need to know why I can't leverage up this wagon. If there's too much weight, nothing's gonna lift it."

Chloe figured with just a horse, he couldn't steal much. The weight of the things in the wagon hadn't occurred to her. No wonder she wasn't able to do anything with it. He was definitely smarter than most men she'd met, even if he was bossy.

"There's the spare wheel, Granny's furniture, two barrels of brine with meat, clothes, pots, pans, linens, books—"

"Shit." He shook his head.

"Granny will tan your damn hide for cussing."

"You shouldn't cast stones. You seem to know a lot of cuss words yourself." He stared at the wagon. "This means we're going to have to empty it."

"Empty it? Whatever for? We can just take some of the stuff off—"

"No, that won't work." He cut her off again. "The broken wheel is on the front of the wagon. My guess is that's where the really heavy stuff is. We have to empty it or it's not going anywhere."

Chloe wanted to rail at him, tell him to leave, but she held her tongue. If she'd have had more sleep and less aggravation, she might have realized the wagon was too heavy to lift.

She sighed. "Fine, then, let's get to emptying it."

His only reply was a grunt and a muttered curse.

It was already midafternoon. No doubt it would be dark by the time they got everything off the wagon. Mr. Blackwood would be spending the night with them. Chloe didn't know if she should be excited or nervous.

Or maybe both.

Chapter Two

"Is this chest made out of lead? Jesus Christ, I think I'm going to need a new back after this one." Gideon thought he'd rip his arms out of their sockets trying to haul the chest out of the back of the wagon.

"No, but it's full of Granny's dishes." The girl said that as if it made perfect sense.

"Goddamn it!" Gideon's voice echoed across the field, where the deepening twilight crept through the tall grass. He winced when he realized just how loud he'd been. No doubt Granny and the little girls had heard him clearly.

"Mr. Blackwood, I don't care how much you cuss around me, but those little girls are innocent as can be." Chloe leaned toward him, sweat rivulets running down her face, hair plastered to her freckled cheeks. She looked wild-eyed and exhausted.

He felt the same way four hours after he'd stopped to help the Ruskin family. The whole afternoon was like quicksand. Every time he moved, he sank farther into the muck. It wasn't Chloe's fault, but damned if he wasn't annoyed as hell with her. She seemed like a smart girl, so why hadn't it occurred to her to empty the weight from the wagon? He was surprised the mules could pull it. Perhaps they were as stubborn as the little fiery-haired woman in front of him.

"Sorry. I'll mind my tongue." He said it grudgingly, but she nodded anyway.

By the time they got the rest of the incredibly well-packed furniture out of the wagon, the sun had set. Gideon knew in a short time he wouldn't be able to see what he was doing. He was good and stuck for the night with the Ruskins.

Fantastic.

"I've got to go get a fire started so we can make supper." Chloe pulled off her hat and wiped her forehead on her dirty sleeve. "Girls are liable to be hungry." She glanced at the horizon. "It'll be dark soon."

Gideon looked at the chaos around him, the scattering of belongings that made up the family's life. It was an achingly familiar sight, one he'd seen more than once after the war. He hadn't had anything to carry with him when he'd left Georgia. He'd traveled with nothing but the Devils, his closest friends and all he needed. These folks had a little left, nothing but scraps to many, yet he knew it was everything to the Ruskins.

On the heels of that thought, his annoyance with them flew away on the breeze. They were simple folks trying to make a new life for themselves as he'd done a few years earlier. He couldn't fault them for being brave enough to leave Virginia for Texas. It was a long, hard journey. The fact that a young woman, an old woman and two small girls were doing it on their own testified to their courage and fortitude.

The least he could do was repair their wheel and get them safely on their way. If nothing else, it would take his mind off Tanger for a day.

"I'll gather some firewood." Gideon's muscles shook with exhaustion as he walked toward the patch of trees. Chloe's gaze nearly burned a hole in his back, which made him twitch. At first, he'd had trouble thinking of her as a woman, and then she'd surprised the hell out of him with a pair of tits his palms itched to touch, to weigh, to squeeze. He clenched his fists to stop the urges. The girl was a mixture of brash innocence and strength, not to mention elemental passion.

She confused him, and he didn't like that one bit. When morning came, he'd be on his way. At that point, he could leave Chloe Ruskin behind for good.

He led his horse over to the mules to hobble him for the night. He didn't quite understand what he was seeing as he approached the animals. Surprise made him stop in his tracks and stare. Would that woman never cease to shock him?

She had tied each of the mules to a lead rope, which was secured to a rope strung between two solid trees. All four mules could wander at least twenty feet with the contraption, including to the small creek just beyond the trees and to the sweet grass around the meadow. Not only did Chloe have guts and grit, she had intelligence and common sense. He'd never met another woman like her.

A little flustered by the continuing surprises, he secured his own gelding with the mules. Gideon spent time making sure all the animals were comfortable, although it wasn't necessary. Chloe's ingenious design already made sure of that.

Gathering firewood in the cool air helped him get his composure back. The fact he'd lost his temper wasn't lost on him. He was not the angry Devil; he was the levelheaded captain everyone looked to for orders and for guidance. Gideon didn't want to be angry, and he was ashamed to admit he didn't know why the woman had set him off. Perhaps it was a combination of his escape from the pressures of everyone in Tanger acting like matchmakers along with his unusual reaction to Chloe.

If only he had Zeke or Jake to talk to. They would let him

rail about the sticky situation. But he was alone, and by his own choice too. Well, not alone really, because he had the entire Ruskin family with him. At least for the next twelve hours anyway.

He wanted to get on his horse and ride like hell out of there, but he wouldn't. Honor compelled him to finish what he started, and leaving the Ruskins in worse shape than he found them would be far from honorable. Gideon washed up in the creek, getting most of the sweat and grime off with sand from the bed. After retrieving a clean shirt to slip on from his saddlebags, he rinsed out the filthy one and hung it on a bush to dry.

By the time he made it over to the fire, he was calmer, if not comfortable with the situation. The murmur of female voices greeted him, and he frowned at the sound. He'd left Tanger to get away from women, and here he was trapped with four females. That was ironic enough to make him choke. The fire was a warm glow in the cool night air and the smell of cooking meat teased his nose. Where the hell had they gotten fresh meat?

Chloe had taken off her hat and secured her hair with something, pulling it away from her face. In the firelight, she looked younger, if that were possible. Her expression reflected the same confusion he'd been feeling all afternoon. Apparently he affected her as much as she affected him.

The two little girls sat like tiny blonde owls, staring at him with wide eyes as they nibbled on food from the same tin plate.

Granny nodded at him. "Mr. Blackwood." She pointed to a log. "Set a spell and have some supper. Chloe snared a couple fat hares."

She was snaring rabbits while he was fiddling with the animals and washing? Well, holy shit, didn't he feel foolish? It was the first time in his life a woman had provided for *him* instead of the other way around. It made his stomach flip once, then twice. He sat down and told himself Chloe was a survivor, nothing more. She did what she needed to stay alive, and that obviously meant providing for her family.

Chloe took care of her grandmother and the two little girls alone, without a man's help. That was a simple truth Gideon had trouble accepting. Women were not providers.

Granny handed him a plate with steaming meat and a piece of cornpone.

"Thank you, Mrs. Ruskin." His stomach yowled noisily.

She grinned, showing a few gaps in her smile. "Call me Granny. Everyone does. A big man like you has to have a big appetite. There's plenty, so eat up."

He realized the girls had used one plate so he could eat with them. Not only that, but it appeared Chloe had caught two rabbits because he was there. The petty way he'd been acting made him feel six inches high. The family needed help, but they did everything they could to make him feel welcome.

Granny sat back down with a groan and a few snaps from her joints. She proceeded to pick up her plate and start eating with her fingers. Gideon was not squeamish about bad table manners or even folks who lacked them, but he'd never seen a woman eat like that. She gummed the meat, then smacked her lips.

He was hard-pressed not to crack a smile. Chloe's glower made him swallow his amusement. The entire family was a bit odd, not that he could cast any stones.

"Where you hail from, stranger?"

"I live in Tanger. It's about half a day's ride west." He took a bite of the cornpone, and a groan popped out of his mouth at the heavenly taste.

"She cooks good, don't she?" Granny grinned at Chloe. "She ain't much to look at it, but Chloe has skills a husband would be pleased to have."

The bite of food almost turned to dust in his mouth. Was he not safe anywhere? He left home to get away from the matchmakers and found one in the middle of nowhere with a busted wagon wheel.

"Granny! Leave the man alone. I don't want a husband, and I know he don't want me as a wife." Chloe's scowl could have scared a pack of wolves away. "Don't be meddling in his life for no good reason but to give yourself a chuckle."

Granny did exactly that, chuckled until it became a guffaw, then a bite of beans snuck out the side of her mouth. As she wiped it away with her fingers, Gideon wondered if some higher power had put these folks in his path for a reason. He'd be damned if he could figure out why, since he was more uncomfortable than he'd felt in a long time.

"He's handsome. He ain't married—wait, you ain't hitched, are ya?" Granny peered at him as if she could tell by counting his eyebrow hairs whether or not he had a wife.

They all stared at him, the only sounds the popping of the fire and Granny's gumming.

"Nope." The word was dragged from the depths of his guts.

The old woman cackled merrily. "See, there you go. If you have a mind to, I'm sure Chloe would be a good one to take to wife."

Chloe stood and dropped her plate on the ground. "That's enough nonsense. I don't *want* to marry him, or any man for that matter. I don't need a man in my life."

She kissed the girls on the tops of their heads and walked toward where the mules were tethered.

"No matter what she says, that girl needs a man in her life. Life ain't enough if you don't find someone to share it with." Granny continued smacking her food.

Gideon's thoughts returned again to why he'd crossed paths with the Ruskins. Did it mean something? Did he want to know the answer to that question? Probably not, since the conversation had turned to marriage within ten minutes, and that was something he was currently running from. He just needed to get the job done and be on his way.

They finished the meal in silence, the chatter and the suggestions of husband material tucked away, thank God. He didn't blame them for looking to him to take care of them. No doubt there'd been plenty of strangers in their path as they made their journey, and likely he was one of few people who helped them. In fact, he was sure some of them had not-so-honorable intentions. The Ruskins would be fools if they trusted him enough to marry Chloe off to him after a twelve-hour acquaintance.

The rabbit was more than delicious. It was exactly what he'd needed after hours of moving freight off the wagon. The cornpone was slightly sweet and melted in his mouth. After living above the restaurant for two years, he'd eaten everything imaginable. This simple meal was the tastiest and most satisfying one he'd had in quite some time. He refused to believe it was because of the company.

Chloe Ruskin was just a girl, a woman who would be gone from his life by this time tomorrow night.

"If'n you feel that strongly about him, you need to follow your heart," Granny whispered. "There ain't many opportunities for a gal to find a strong man, one who stirs her inside."

Chloe's heart lodged in her throat, beating madly as she

stared at her grandmother. She had done many things in her life she wished she could undo. There had been no time to consider the consequences. That excuse wouldn't work, because now it was her deliberate choice and she was scared witless.

She liked Gideon, although she'd not admit it to him. He was a handsome man who made her body feel things she'd not known existed. She'd been carrying around her virginity, and it had become a damn burden, especially for a woman without a man to protect her. Many times she'd been threatened by men on the trail, and it was only blind luck no one had lived up to their threats. Chloe wanted to get rid of her virginal state, and Gideon was a man who could not only accomplish that task, but she was drawn to him. More so than any other man she'd met in her life. Yet this would be giving herself to a man she barely knew, a man she would never see again.

"Granny, I'm scared."

"What are you scared of?"

"What if he doesn't want me?" Chloe managed to say. "I ain't pretty, and I sure don't know how to please a man."

Granny waved her hand. "Ain't nothing to it, girl. Grab hold of his man part until it gets hard and stick it inside you. He'll take it from there."

The crude words made her flinch. Her grandmother was outspoken, and sometimes it was too much to absorb.

"I don't know if I can."

"With all the menfolk who've tried to bed you the last few years, you're being shy now? You're the one who told me what you was fixin' to do." Granny pulled her blanket closer around her.

Unfamiliar emotions nearly overwhelmed her—she normally didn't allow anything soft to surface. "I want to bed him. That's the bald truth. I've been looking for the right man, and he is near about perfect."

Granny shrugged. "You ain't never gonna marry. Why you holding on to your virginity? There ain't no way you got your virgin veil inside after riding a horse every day for nearly twenty years. Mr. Blackwood won't notice the difference." Granny's coarse argument was logical. "I ain't gonna tell you not to, because that never works. It's your choice now."

Young men, even old men, were few and far between since the war. A grand specimen like Gideon Blackwood was rare as a blue moon. As a child, Chloe had always thought there would be a man for her. Now as a woman who had hit plenty of rough patches in her life, she wanted to survive to be a seventy-year-old curmudgeon. Life hadn't yet presented her with a man who stirred her, made her want things, want him. Until now.

She got to her feet and blew out a breath. The moon illuminated the path across the meadow to the wagon where he slept. It was a hundred yards, but it could have been a hundred miles. By far the longest walk she'd ever take.

As Chloe made her way to the wagon across the dew-covered tall grass, she clenched and unclenched her hands. There were many reasons Gideon could reject her, starting with her plain looks, her short stature, her overly curvy behind, the abundant freckles, not to mention her big mouth and enormous dose of pride. She was no catch for a man like him. He made it clear he didn't want a wife, or her, for that matter.

Chloe might get pregnant, but she could tell folks she was a widow. The last thing she needed was another young'un though. The girls were more than a handful—Chloe didn't want to contemplate how much work a new baby would be for their lopsided family.

Chloe accepted the raw truth. With this action, she would

be taking advantage of Gideon Blackwood and giving him nothing in return except a good meal and some pleasure. Her heart fluttered like a trapped butterfly while the rest of her tingled with anticipation. She didn't understand her reaction but followed her natural instincts, which told her to bed him, no matter what.

By the time she got to the wagon, Chloe shook hard enough to make her teeth rattle. She closed her eyes and took deep, slow breaths. She had been attracted to him from the moment she'd seen him walking toward the wagon. He was the one she wanted to lose her virginity with, the man to show her what it meant to be a woman. With a lean-hipped swagger that reminded her of a large cat, soft brown curls and blue eyes, his appeal seemed endless.

She had to do this. She would do this.

Chloe climbed into the wagon.

Gideon was having a highly enjoyable dream. In it, a woman had slid up next to him in bed. She was warm and soft, slowly caressing his chest and arms. His dick began to respond to her ministrations, and he moaned at the pleasure from just her touch. She smelled good, like sunshine and woman.

He reached for her and noted she was shaking. "It's okay, darling. Come closer and I'll warm you up."

She sighed against his shoulder, and that's when he knew he wasn't dreaming at all. There was a woman in his arms, and he was sleeping in a wagon.

"Chloe?"

"I'm lonely. I need to feel a man's touch again." Her words were rushed, and she sounded nervous.

Gideon came fully awake when her words sank in. Chloe

wanted to lie with him. In the wagon. In the cold. Could this day be any stranger?

"Please, Gideon. I-I just thought we could make each other feel g-good." She reached for his trousers, and he stopped her.

"Chloe, I can't bed you in this wagon with your grandmother within hearing distance."

To his surprise, she shook her head. "Don't you worry about Granny. She knows I have needs."

Chloe pushed his hands away and took hold of his still semi-hard dick. To his chagrin, he hardened completely, pulsing against her palm. Who was he to push her away? She said she wanted to be with a man again. Obviously she had sexual experience, and he could appreciate being lonely. He was lonely every day of his life, even with his family around him.

Her movements were awkward, but her hand was magic. She stroked him up and down, tugging with each pass. He closed his eyes and reveled in the feel of her small hand and dexterous fingers. It was a spectacular way to wake up.

When she climbed on top of him and pulled off her dress, she didn't have ladies' drawers on or those hideous pants she'd sported earlier. Chloe was naked as the day she was born under that potato sack. Her alabaster skin nearly glowed in the half light. He couldn't help but reach out and touch her warm thighs. They were firm but softer than anything he'd touched before.

They were also trembling.

A terrible thought occurred to him. "Chloe, are you doing this because you think you owe me something?"

"No, I'm doing this because I want to. I owe *me* something."

He didn't understand her response, and before he could formulate another question, she slid down his erection. Her pussy was so tight, it was like a fist inside her. Yet he was embedded in only moments. He quietly blew out a breath of relief that she wasn't a virgin.

But she was so fucking snug, she couldn't have had much experience. Then there was her awkward attempt at riding him, which was clumsy enough he took pity on her. He flipped her on her back in one swift movement, leaving them face-to-face. Her breath came in choppy bursts, the heat bathing his skin.

He pulled out, then slid back in slowly, reveling in the feel of her sweet pussy. Gideon focused on the two things he'd been thinking about all evening—her tits. He couldn't quite tell the nipple color, but it was light, likely pink. The nipples were currently hard and pointing straight at him. He reached down and lapped at them, earning a surprised moan from Chloe. Whoever she'd been with previously must not have seen to her pleasure. The least Gideon could do was show her what she'd been missing.

While his mouth closed around the right breast, one hand closed around the left. She gasped, and her body arched up to meet him. Gideon decided her breasts were exactly the right size, enough to fill his hands and mouth, perfect. She was so responsive to him, even pulling at his back and thrusting up at him, but he kept his measured pace.

Little did she know, Gideon was forcing himself to go slowly. She was tight enough to make him come within seconds. If he didn't control himself, he'd pound into her until he couldn't see straight. Then all of it would be over much too quickly. He wanted to take his time.

When he bit down on her nipple, she hissed and clenched around his dick. She liked it, so he did it to the other sweet breast. This time she scratched him as her fingers dug into his shoulders.

"You like that, little one?"

She responded by tightening around his cock, which should've been impossible, but it happened anyway. That was like putting a lit match in dry tinder, because the orgasm roared through him. He didn't even have time to warn her to hold on. Instead he sucked and bit at her nipples, seeing stars behind his closed lids as intense pleasure coursed through him. He at least tried to remember not to crush Chloe, but he could hardly see straight, much less think. When he rolled off her, she sighed.

"Sorry about that. I meant to hold back but, uh, I couldn't." His voice was a hoarse whisper in the quiet of the night.

"It's okay. Men just do their business and move on. It ain't nothing to apologize for."

Her sweeping statement pricked Gideon's pride. Even if it was true, he didn't want to be lumped in with other men, maybe even those who had used her to "do their business". Truthfully, he was a considerate lover, most of the time. He hadn't been with a woman in over a year, and this nighttime tryst had sent him over the edge like a shooting star.

"No, it's not okay. I meant to see to your pleasure." He rolled onto his side and plucked one nipple. "If you'll let me, I'll do it now."

"Do what?"

Gideon smiled and leaned down to kiss her. She looked up at him in confusion. He realized she had no idea that women could get pleasure from sex with men. He was going to change that misconception.

"I'm going to make you feel good too."

"You gonna lick my titties again? I liked that." She was definitely as brash in bed as she was out.

Without answering her, he reached for the beautiful tits and began making Chloe feel good. She made kittenish moans as he slowly licked all around the nipples, avoiding the tips until she tugged at his hair. Smiling, he pinched one turgid peak and nibbled at the other.

"Oh my."

Gideon skimmed his hand down her soft belly until he reached the crinkly hairs between her legs. Damp with their combined juices, his fingers slid into her folds easily. She sucked in a breath when he found her clit.

"What are you doing?"

"Relax, little one. I'm making you feel good." He could tell she'd never experienced the truest pleasure a human being could find.

As he lapped at one nipple then the other, she clenched at his shoulder. Her heart beat against his cheek, hard and fast. As perspiration coated her skin, her breath grew choppy. He knew she was close to finding her release. He rubbed his fingers faster on the swollen bud of pleasure. She arched her back as her entire body tightened. A keening cry, softer than an owl's hoot, slipped from her lips.

"God in heaven." She sucked in a shaky breath. "What was that?"

He kissed her and tucked her under his arm. "That was pleasure."

"I think I'd like to do that again."

Gideon chuckled and kissed her forehead. "I don't mind giving a lady what she asks for, but we're not going to do that again."

"Are you sure?" Her voice was the softest he'd heard all day.

"Yes, I'm sure." The last thing Gideon wanted was to be involved with Chloe any more than he already was. If he'd been more awake when she'd first crawled into the wagon, he would have told her no. Done was done, though, but he wasn't going to repeat it.

Chloe held back tears through force of will. She'd never, *ever* felt anything like what Gideon had just done with her. It was incredible, amazing, beyond the stars in the sky. Granny hadn't said anything about how she'd feel or the way her body would nearly explode in his hands.

She lay there and listened to his heartbeat against her ear. He was a warm man, handsome and skilled in bed play. Any girl would be happy to have him as her mate.

Even Chloe.

Oh, she didn't pretend it would ever happen, but it was nice to think about for a little while. He didn't take her seriously as a woman, but he did treat her as one in the darkness of the wagon. He'd taught her a lot, and she couldn't regret he'd been the one to take her virginity, although he would never know what he'd done.

Chloe waited until his breathing became even and she was sure he was asleep. She didn't want to leave him. He was warmer than a fire, and damned if she wasn't comfortable as all get-out snuggled up against him. With a sigh, she pulled herself away and dressed. As she crept out of the wagon silently, she could smell his scent on her skin, could still feel the ghosts of his hands on her body.

When she was far enough away, she let a few tears fall. She would allow herself to grieve for what could have been, but only for a little while. There was no time for more than that.

Gideon woke as if someone had pinched him. He sat up, noting his trousers were unbuttoned and the sun was almost up. As he rubbed his hands down his cheeks, the unmistakable scent of a woman on his fingers slapped him across the face.

Jesus Christ.

He'd allowed Chloe to crawl into his bed, then had lost control five minutes later. What the hell had he been thinking? Well, he hadn't been thinking at all. He'd been half-awake and in a perpetual state of horniness. Gideon had been attracted to Chloe the day before, and his weak will had succumbed to a woman's touch on his dick.

He dressed quickly, stuffing his shirt into his trousers, careful not to let his hands come near the organ that had betrayed him too easily. Gideon jumped out of the wagon, glancing at the campsite and noting the ladies were already up and about. Damn.

He walked toward the creek to wash. Chloe's scent on his hands was more than distracting. He knew she'd come to him—it had been her choice. Yet he could have said no, could have pushed her away. He hadn't, of course, and he didn't want to think about why. Gideon was supposed to be getting away from women, not pulling the first one he met into his bed. Granny would likely shoot off his dick if she knew what he'd been up to with her granddaughter.

Gideon was disappointed with his self-control. After all the postulating he'd done in Tanger to his family, he did exactly the opposite of what he'd intended. He washed his hands with sand until they were reddened from the grit and the cold-as-hell water.

After splashing water on his face, he smashed his hat on his head and headed back to the wagon. He would forget breakfast, even if he wanted coffee bad enough his teeth hurt.

The wagon needed to get fixed and as fast as possible. As he marched across the meadow, he heard Chloe call his name, but he kept going.

Gideon was ready to get busy, and nothing she said was going to stop him. She reached the wagon seconds after he did, demonstrating just how fast she was. Chloe was wearing the potato-sack dress again and the floppy hat. She put her hands on her hips.

"Ready to get started?" She pointed to the stump he'd hauled over to prop up the wagon. "I can roll it under when you've got the wagon up."

Gideon peered at her, although he could hardly see her eyes in the shadow of the damn hat. "Are you okay?"

It was as close as he'd come to telling her he felt guilty about what they'd done. He wanted to apologize but figured she would take it as an insult.

"I'm fine. Why wouldn't I be? I already had my breakfast." Her annoyed tone told him she was back to normal. Must be she had conquered whatever had driven her to seek him out in the darkness.

"Then let's get going. I want to be on my way at some point today. No point in staying another night."

Gideon was embarrassed to hear the words spill out of his mouth, more so when she flinched. He'd never acted such a way toward a woman, especially one he'd already been intimate with. He had been rude and, to his chagrin, downright mean to the point where his mother would have blistered his ears had she been alive to do it. When he opened his mouth to apologize, she cut him off before he had a chance to squeak out one syllable.

"Stop flapping your gums if you're in such a hurry. Let's get the wheel fixed." She pushed one stump onto its side and rolled it to the wagon, then repeated it with the second stump she had found on her own. He should have thought to use two, but he was rapidly discovering his brain ceased to work normally when Chloe was around.

Gideon took a moment to swallow back the curses stuck in his throat before he picked up the branch he'd found to lever up the wagon. He had a hard time reconciling the tiny dictator in front of him with the woman who had crawled into his bed six hours earlier. An even harder time not asking her outright why she was so dang ornery.

Time to get the Ruskins on their way.

He jammed the branch under the wagon, the rock serving as the fulcrum, digging into the dirt to get a better lift. She rolled the stump to the middle and waited by his feet. In contrast to the wagon, she was small and vulnerable. If he lost his grip, she could be injured or even crushed. The responsibility of her welfare was on his shoulders, and it made him itch all over. He'd shouldered many responsibilities in his life, but over the last few years had been left with only one—the restaurant he ran with his cousin. Gideon was a natural leader, and folks usually followed along behind him. Now he'd run across the one woman who not only didn't want to follow him, she wanted to lead herself. And she likely didn't appreciate being at his feet.

With a mighty heave, he levered the wagon up. The strain forced a primal roar out of his mouth that echoed around them. Within seconds, Chloe had one stump then the other wedged under the wagon and had scooted away.

"I'm clear."

Although he wanted to drop it, Gideon slowly lowered the wagon, hearing every pop and creak the wood made. By the time the thing was resting on the stumps, he was shaking and sweating. Chloe thumped each one and then looked up at him.

"I guess it worked." She rose and peered at him. "Appears you need some vittles after all. I'll get the wheel off while you go get yourself some breakfast."

"I'm not leaving you here to take off that wheel alone." The very idea made his temper rise. "What kind of man do you think I am?"

"One who just levered up that wagon by himself. I ain't never seen the like." Chloe sounded impressed. "Now get some food in you. Taking off the wheel ain't no big job."

Gideon was a little flustered by her assessment of him. It took him a few moments to recover. "I'd rather you wait. That wagon could come down on you, and where would Granny and the girls be without you?" He pointed at the new wheel propped up at the other side of the wagon. "If you want to do something, grease up the new wheel and the axles."

She wanted to tell him to go to hell, he could see it in her face, but she merely shrugged and snatched up the bucket that had pine tar in it. The woman was testing his patience, stomping on his last nerve—no doubt he was having the same effect on her. Gideon could attribute the passion between them for the incredible sex they'd shared in the wagon. That passion obviously would lead to nothing but trouble for either of them.

He walked toward the others, feeling the burn of Chloe's stare on his back again. It was as sharp as her tongue. Granny stood at the fire, wooden spoon in hand and a frown on her face to match her granddaughter's. Yep, the Ruskins definitely needed to be on their way.

"What kinda fool starts his work without a good meal under his belt?"

The two little moppets sat on the same log as the night before, chewing on what appeared to be jerky. They stared at him without blinking, which spooked him just a bit.

"The kinda fool who wants everyone to get going to where they need to be." He sat down and reached for the coffee pot. Granny rapped his knuckles with the spoon.

"That's powerful hot, and we don't need no burns to add to our troubles." She used the apron, which he noticed was thin enough he could see her hand through it, to pour him a cup of coffee. "I've got cornpone from last night and some jerky. Ain't got no sugar to speak of, but the coffee is hot."

"That's all I need. I'm mighty grateful for it too." He accepted a plate with a huge piece of cornpone and a few stringy-looking pieces of jerky. The family barely had enough to feed themselves and here they were giving him two meals' worth of food in one. "I can't take this much."

"We only got a few hundred miles to go. Asides, we cain't pay you for your help, and a Ruskin always settles their debt." She said something to the girls low enough for him to miss, and they scurried off toward the creek.

Gideon's mouth dried up as he wondered if the wooden spoon was about to crack him over the head. What if Chloe had told her grandmother about their midnight sex? What if Granny pulled out a shotgun and pointed it at his head? Was he ready to make a lifetime commitment to a girl he barely knew?

"Cornpone is good." He avoided looking at the older woman, hoping like hell she would simply start cleaning up or begin some other chore. Her stare was more powerful than the coffee, for pity's sake.

"Chloe made it. I cain't cook much no more with the pains in my fingers. She learned all her female skills along with the man ones like hunting." Granny sat down with her own cup of coffee and continued to stare at him. "You like her?"

Gideon choked on the food, nearly sucking a big piece of it

into his lungs. Granny pounded on his back while his eyes watered and his lungs ached for air. He finally got a breath in and swallowed the rest of the bite. He gulped some hot coffee, partially soothing his battered throat.

"Don't go and die on me now. You're too big to hoist into the wagon to get you to an undertaker, and we don't have no shovel to bury you." Granny sat back down and eyeballed him some more. "You like her?" she repeated.

This time Gideon was ready for the question. "Chloe?"

"Yes, Chloe. Don't play stupid with me, Mr. Blackwood."

He thought about how to answer her and again wondered if she knew about the shenanigans in the wagon. "She's strong, smart and full of pride. Her mouth is sharper than an axe, and she's ornery as the mules she tends."

To his surprise, Granny smiled. "Good. You do like her."

"I never said that."

"You didn't have to. I can read it in your eyes when you talk about her." Granny cackled like a seasoned witch. "I'll be damned."

Apparently, so would Gideon.

Bossy, that's what he was. Bossy and demanding. Chloe was trying to think of better words for Gideon as she greased up the axles, but she didn't have much in the way of book learning to draw from. He drove her to cussing beneath the dang wagon while he sat there with Granny and ate the vittles Chloe had made.

He'd practically run the other direction from her when he finally emerged from the wagon. Heck, he hadn't even looked at her as he headed toward the creek. Obviously, her skills under the sheets were not only forgettable, they were enough to send a man running. Chloe had made the choice to be with him and wouldn't regret it, no matter what. Gideon was likely wishing she hadn't, but that was too damn bad. There was no way to unring that bell. Chloe was no longer a virgin.

Granny had always been worried Chloe's first time would be with some cowpoke or drifter raping her. It gave her a certain satisfaction to know she had chosen when and with whom to lose her untouched status. It was an experience she could easily get used to if he was her husband. The very thought of actually marrying Gideon made her snort so hard, she almost sucked in a lungful of tar.

"You need some help, little one?"

She rolled her eyes at his question. "Greasing up an axle is easy, remember?" She crawled from beneath the wagon with the bucket in one hand and a handful of grease in the other. "My fingers can manage to grease up a stick."

As soon as she realized what she said, as well as the state of her hand, Chloe's cheeks heated. She never, *ever* blushed, and now that she'd given herself to this stranger, her cheeks heated too easily. Thinking about greasing up a stick next to the very wagon in which she'd touched his stick embarrassed her.

Gideon looked at her hands, and for just a moment she felt the heat from it; then he turned away so fast he kicked up a cloud of dust with his boots. She didn't know whether to throw the grease at him or make him kiss her.

What had being with him done to her?

"I'll, uh, get started on the wheel now." He tugged on the lug bolt she'd greased and kept his back to her.

Chloe wiped the leftover grease on her hand back into the bucket and used a rag to get her fingers mostly clean. The trip from Virginia had been rough and hard, but that was the physical side of it. The long hours, the constant danger from everyone and everything, the fear for the future, all of that came crashing down on Chloe, and she sat down in the dirt heavily.

Gideon continued to ignore her, which suited her just fine. He didn't need to see her struggling to find her bearings. She didn't like emotions and all the confusion they caused. If only she hadn't found what she wanted but couldn't keep—Gideon. After a minute or two of pure self-pity and stupidity, she mentally pulled herself up by her drawers and got on her feet. Sooner the wheel got swapped, the sooner she could leave him behind.

Of course when she glanced at him, he was squatting, and she had to notice his behind was nicely muscled, quite perfect. Then she noticed his shoulders were nearly as wide as the damn wheel.

Hell and crackers. What was wrong with her?

She knelt by the other wheels and checked to make sure they were greased enough, anything to keep her mind from acting loco. Gideon was only a few feet away, and every movement he made, from his breath to his grunts, echoed across her skin. She was ready to give up and run like a coward, and since she was already a fool, running wasn't going to make her look any less foolish.

He pushed the new wheel on and spread the grease on the axle, sliding his hands on the shaft as the wheel moved into place. Chloe watched his movement, mesmerized by his long, strong fingers. She knew their touch firsthand. It was a good thing all she had to do was wait for him to finish and wipe her hands clean.

He finished securing the lug bolt and turned to her. "Rag?"

Chloe threw it at him rather than get close enough to hand it to him. Unfortunately it hit him square in the face. She winced inwardly but didn't apologize. He wasn't being particularly nice either so it served him right to get a little dirty.

"Thanks, little one. That was mighty nice of you." His sarcasm was sharper than the knife in her boot.

"Anytime. I'm always willing to help out a fellow human being."

Gideon grunted and threw the rag back at her. She tried to snatch it from the air, but it ended up on her hat instead. He made a choking noise like he was holding in a laugh. She narrowed her eyes and took off her hat. A huge stain from the grease marked the top, which would be impossible to remove.

"You ruined it."

This time he snorted out loud. "That hat was ruined long before I got here."

"It was a perfectly good hat and cost me nothing. I found it on our way out of Virginia."

"Then the previous owner had smarts enough to leave it behind."

"You're not being nice."

"Neither are you." He rose to his feet, and she did too, even if she only reached his chin.

"Let's get this done, then, and you can be on your way, Mr. Blackwood. Obviously the company ain't fitting for a man with such good taste." She would never let him know how much his comments hurt, made her feel he was looking down his nose at her. After all, he was a highfalutin stranger, and she was the daughter of a dirt farmer with nothing but a broken-down wagon, an old woman and two little girls.

Gideon and Chloe worked in awkward silence from then on. He levered up the wagon, and she got the stumps out from underneath quickly. He let the wagon down slowly, his muscles straining with each inch. She found herself again entranced by the way his body moved—the strength of his arms and shoulders astounded her. While she wanted to be angry with him, her body betrayed her head completely.

When the wagon was finally on all four wheels again, it let loose a mighty wooden groan. Chloe whooped and threw her greasy hat in the air. After being stuck for nearly a week, they'd be on their way that day. For the first time in a while, she experienced a rush of happiness, and it was all due to Gideon Blackwood.

Chloe threw her arms around him and whooped again. He twirled her around, and somehow his mouth landed on hers. The celebratory kiss made her toes curl.

Then Granny shouted her name with clear panic in her voice.

Gideon dropped her to her feet with a horrified look on his face. She turned and ran toward her grandmother. Granny never panicked, *never*. The older woman stood alone at the campfire, wringing her hands. Chloe ran faster—Granny also never wrung her hands.

"What's wrong?"

"It's the girls. They weren't back from washing their hands ten minutes ago. I went to find them, and they're gone."

Chloe's mouth went dry. Those girls were young and innocent. They likely wandered off and got lost. "I'll find them. Probably lost their way." As she walked toward the woods, Granny grabbed her arm.

"They ain't lost. There's boot prints and horse tracks all around the bank. Somebody took them."

Chloe's heart dropped to her feet. "What do you mean somebody took them?"

"I ain't a tracker, but I know what the bank looked like this morning, and there wasn't any tracks like that." Granny looked to Gideon. "You have any tracking skills?"

"Not as good as my cousin, but I've a fair amount. I'll find them." He took off running toward the woods.

Chloe was right on his heels. There was no way she was going to let him find those girls without her.

The Ruskin quagmire kept getting deeper. Just as soon as he'd fixed the damn wagon, the little moppets disappeared. Gideon wanted to get to Nate's, but he was pulled in again to help the little family. The girls were innocent, of course, unless they engineered their own disappearance, which was ridiculous. Even the most devious five-year-old could not create horseshoe tracks or man-sized shoeprints in the mud in ten minutes.

More than likely, if they'd seen strangers, the girls would have hidden somewhere. Maybe got lost on their way back to the campfire. Hopefully he'd find them in a short time and then get the wagon loaded so the Ruskins could be on their way and he could continue on his journey.

Life, however, never seemed to follow the most logical path, even if he wished for it hard enough his head ached. He heard Chloe running behind him, which he expected, of course. The strong-willed woman would not allow anything to happen that she didn't have control over. She was like a short version of himself. He let loose a snort at the thought—she was nothing like him beneath the potato-sack dress, that was for sure.

He needed to focus on the task at hand and not the confusing, enticing Chloe Ruskin and the memory of her lips on his five minutes ago. Hell, he could still taste her, and fool that he was, he licked his lips, making his dick twitch.

Focus, Captain, focus.

Gideon hit the woods with a good head of steam. The smell of the loamy earth surrounded him. The leaves on the sun-dappled forest floor muffled the sound of his boots. He heard the water burbling ahead and took the path the girls had likely followed. It was the most direct route. When he was twenty feet away, he slowed down, and Chloe plowed into his back, nearly knocking him over.

"Why are you stopping?" she whispered harshly, then poked him in the back.

"Ouch. I'm stopping because we need to be sure there's no one up there waiting for us. Now either shut up and stay behind me, or go back to your grandmother." His tone was hard as stone. She needed to understand there was possible danger ahead.

She grunted in response, but she remained quiet and kept behind him. He would have stopped to think about the fact she obeyed his order, but there were other problems he needed to focus on.

Gideon closed his eyes and listened carefully. He heard only the sounds of the forest, from birds to squirrels to the creek. There was nothing larger than a rodent moving or breathing.

The silence lasted sixty seconds before she leaned forward and whispered, "What are you doing?"

"Listening, now shush." Gideon's tone hopefully told her to shut up as politely as he could.

He studied the ground in front of him, noting the broken branches, the small impressions in leaves on the soft soil beneath. These were signs of the girls, not an adult. He crept forward, very conscious of the woman nearly in his back pocket. Her body heat permeated his clothes all down his back. For such a small woman, she sure did generate a lot of warmth. He gritted his teeth and ignored the sensation.

As they crept closer to the creek, he slowed even further, looking at every sign left behind by the humans and animals that had come through. Five feet from the bank, there was a deep shoe impression on top of one of the girls' shoe prints. Gideon's heart did a flip at the sight—Granny had been right. Someone had been there besides them.

It was a single man, and his foot was just a little smaller than Gideon's, definitely an adult. He favored the left side of his foot, as the impression was deeper on the right. Not many men walked in such a way, which should make it easier to find him. Probably was a bit pigeon-toed, if Gideon wasn't mistaken.

He went around the footprint, noting another three before he reached the creek. That's where the mud got thicker, and everything mixed together. Near as he could tell, the girls were on their haunches washing their hands when the man walked up behind them. There had been a struggle, and then he had jumped across the creek, making a much deeper impression.

The stranger had been carrying the girls.

He waded through the creek to the other side and saw clear evidence of two horses just beyond the edge of the prints.

The stranger had also not been alone.

Gideon's fists clenched as he glanced back at Chloe. She didn't appear scared or lost. In fact, she looked furious.

"Which way did they go?" Her harsh question scratched at his ears.

Gideon gestured north, where the tracks led. "They went that way, and there were two of them, likely both men. I'm going to get my horse and follow them."

"Not without me, you're not." Chloe pointed at him. "They're my family, not yours."

He didn't answer her, because the idea of her accompanying him was absurd. She had no horse, and his gelding couldn't carry both of them at the speed he intended to ride. Gideon jumped across the water and headed back to the campsite.

"Don't believe for one minute that I don't know what you're thinking. I can ride one of the mules—they're faster than you think." Chloe was taking two steps for every one of his, and she kept up without breaking stride. She was a fast little thing, even if her mule wasn't.

"You need to stay here with your granny and wait for them to come back."

"And you honestly believe those girls are gonna appear out of nowhere? They got taken, and you and I both know it." She ran ahead of him, her arms pumping, skirt flapping, her wild hair flying like a banner behind her.

Gideon tried to catch up, but she had too much of a lead on him. She was fast, darting through the trees like a wood nymph. Although she was short, Chloe was a creature of grace when she ran. It sure as hell wasn't the right time, but he appreciated the sight. He dug deep and found a burst of speed to catch up to her. Soon they were running dangerously fast on slippery, leaf-covered ground. For some absurd reason, he felt like grinning.

What the hell was he doing? Two little girls were missing, and he was playing games with Chloe. He shook off his own foolish behavior and refocused on the problem—finding the girls. When he and Chloe came out of the woods and into the clearing, he stopped short and stared.

Holy God.

The wagon, his horse and Granny Ruskin were gone.

Chapter Three

Chloe's heart squeezed so tightly she could hardly catch her breath. In a matter of minutes, her entire family had disappeared. Was someone playing a cruel trick on her? The remnants of their life, the contents of the wagon, lay where they'd been stacked the day before in the grass. The campfire still burned, the coffee pot sat nearby, yet Granny was gone, as was the newly repaired wagon and Gideon's horse. They'd left everything exactly as it laid waiting to be loaded, like a house had emptied itself and flown away into the bright blue sky.

A wave of anger welled inside her. Their journey hadn't been perfect, but nothing had gone too terribly wrong until now, until Gideon Blackwood rode up to "save" them. Maybe he orchestrated the entire thing and was now planning on getting rid of her to make it complete.

"Where the hell is she?" Chloe had never been more furious in her life.

Gideon frowned at her. "How would I know? I was with you in the woods. In case you haven't noticed, my horse is gone too."

"You took them. Got into my drawers, distracted me and took my family, you bastard." Red fury coated her vision as she stared at the man who may have destroyed all she had. No way would she accept the loss though. If she was anything, Chloe was a fighter, and she would fight for her tiny family. With a roar, she launched herself at him, taking him by surprise. She knocked him to the ground, and they rolled in the tall grass.

Snarling and snapping at him, Chloe tried her best to reach the knife in her boot; that way she could make him talk. However, he was too fast and knocked her hands aside so she didn't have the chance.

"What are you doing?" He successfully grabbed her right hand, but she squirmed free. "Chloe, stop! I didn't do anything to your family."

"Yes, you did. Nothing happened until you got here."

"That's enough." Gideon had apparently been trying not to hurt her, because in a split second, she was facedown in the grass with her arm twisted behind her and his knee resting on her back.

She had never experienced such fear and anger as she did at that moment. Alone in the Texas prairie with a stranger, one she'd bedded but a stranger still, Chloe was helpless. Her heart thumped so hard it hurt, and her breath came in short bursts. After a second or two of panic, Chloe reached down deep and found her determination, then let it loose. She wouldn't stand for his bullying, not for an instant.

"Let me up," she said through gritted teeth.

"Not unless you stop acting loco." He was barely winded, the son of a bitch.

"Tell me where they are." She tried to break his grip, but the man was obviously made of oak. She succeeded in almost breaking her own arm though.

"Stop moving or you're going to hurt yourself."

Chloe barked a laugh. "You've already done enough to hurt me."

"I'm not trying to hurt you. Hell, I spent an entire day helping you. I do have honor, whether or not you believe that right now." He eased his knee up. "I don't know what happened to the wagon, my horse, the girls or Granny, but I promise you, I will find out." She was surprised to hear sincerity in his voice along with a fierceness she hadn't expected.

"Why should I believe you?" As the haze of anger faded, Chloe recognized she needed Gideon. Not only was she a woman alone, but she had no transportation—easy pickings for anyone with less-than-honorable intentions.

"I have no reason to lie to you." He let her loose and stepped back, watching her. There was a stillness about him, as if he could have her on the ground again in seconds if he chose. Likely without much effort judging by how powerful and fast he had been.

It stuck in her craw. Chloe did not like being at anyone's mercy.

She sat up and brushed her hair out of her eyes. "You have no reason to tell the truth either."

"True enough, but I promise you, I did nothing to those girls or Granny, and I sure as hell didn't make the wagon or my damn horse vanish." He put his hands on his hips and looked around the clearing. "If you promise not to try to kill me again, I can track them."

"I wasn't trying to kill you," she mumbled as she got to her feet. If she killed him, she might not find out what happened to Granny and the girls.

Gideon crossed his arms. "I think you would have if you could have, but I can respect that. Family is important to me too."

She brushed off most of the dirt and grass from her skirt. Gideon should have scared her. He was big, strong and fast, and could overpower her. Yet she wasn't afraid of him; she was afraid of never finding her family. She'd never admit it to him, but she did believe he had honor, that he would help her and, grudgingly, that she shouldn't have accused him of wrongdoings. Unless he had a hidden partner, there was no way he could have done any of it. She wasn't about to apologize, though—it might kill her to try.

"Get to tracking." Chloe's throat tightened as she walked toward the campfire.

"We need supplies. If we go after them with nothing but the clothes on our backs, we won't last more than a day."

"Maybe they only have a day." Chloe didn't want to add they might only have hours. The very thought made her want to vomit.

Gideon looked like an immoveable wall of man. "We are no good to them unless we're ready. We have no water, no food. Hell, we don't even have something to lie on to sleep." He pointed at the furniture. "I'm guessing there are linens and such. We've got five minutes to see if we can make some packs to carry what's left of the supplies. Maybe we can even find a blanket or two if we're lucky. Go clean up the supplies by the fire while I search for things we can use. Five minutes, no longer."

"You give too many orders."

He had turned away, heading toward what was left of her family's goods, but he must have heard her anyway, because his shoulders stiffened. "Maybe you ought to follow some."

Chloe wanted to tear off after Granny and the girls, but she knew he was right. Emotion had gotten in her way, more like overwhelmed her. She'd never been so scared in her life, even when she'd been in danger. Those girls had been through a lot. Although they were a handful, they deserved a loving home and a family. They sure as hell didn't deserve to be kidnapped and have awful things done to them.

That was what was making her mind whirl—what might be happening to her family while she cleaned up the coffee pot and dishes. She used sand to wipe off the remnants of breakfast, trying not to think of which one of the girls had made that very mess. Chloe would *not* cry over this. She would be strong and smart, with or without Gideon's help.

Gideon searched through the furniture piece by piece. He focused on the task itself, not on why he was doing it. Admitting he allowed someone to steal two children, an old woman, a wagon with four mules and his horse right out from under his protection was almost incomprehensible. He was one of the most decorated captains in the Confederate army, led so many raids he lost count and had survived four years of hell on earth.

Now he'd lost an entire family while he had been thinking about the woman he'd bedded the night before.

Shame mixed with anger and frustration. The last day had left him with a bad taste in his mouth for more than one reason. Everything had gone horribly wrong, and he had to take responsibility for that. He was a trained soldier with enough sense to control himself. Yet he'd thrown all that away, forgotten who he was and who he should be, all because of his weakness for a tiny curmudgeon with freckles and a big mouth.

Gideon ached to be back in Tanger at the restaurant, doing nothing but enjoying the coffee and the company. He couldn't even go back to Tanger for help. If they didn't get moving and soon, they'd lose the trail and possibly those girls. They had no choice but to follow and hope like hell they didn't find themselves completely outnumbered. If Gideon could get to a telegraph office, he could have four Devils by his side in less than a day. But for now, he had to go on a mission without his friends to help him.

He reached down deep in himself and searched for that iron control, that which made him who he was, what he was. There hadn't been a dangerous situation in his life he hadn't been able to conquer. Chloe had stolen some of the thunder from within him, how he had no idea, but he needed to find it again. He had to ignore his foolish obsession with the woman and clamp down on his wayward emotions until he regained control of them. Their lives depended on it.

More focused, he was able to search faster. In a chest, he found two blankets, a quilted bag, a burlap sack and a leather pouch they might be able to use for water.

Chloe walked up beside him and noted the pile of goods. "Let me take that quilted bag and pack up the cooking supplies. There's some flour, coffee and jerky. Everything else is gone." Her voice was tighter than a tick's ass but not emotional. Thank God. He needed her to stop fussing and start helping.

"Are there sewing notions anywhere?"

She shook her head. "Sewing kit is under the wagon seat, wherever the hell that is."

"Shit. That will make things difficult. I'm going to tear up one of these sheets, if you don't mind, to make straps for a sack."

"They ain't doing me no good. They were Granny's mother's anyway. God knows I ain't slept on 'em." She didn't even look at the linens. In fact, she kept her gaze somewhere over his left shoulder.

He held up the ancient canteen he'd found hidden in one of the drawers, no bigger than his hand. "I came across one thing to carry water, but it's not much. Do you know if there's anything else hidden in here?" He glanced around at the furniture.

She shook her head. "Granny packed most of this. I never even saw that canteen before."

"Then make sure you check the barrels for anything useable. I'll get started making a sack and fill the canteen."

With a nod, she went back to the fire with the bag in her hand. Gideon imagined she was complaining about his highhandedness. Too bad. If they had any chance of catching whoever took her family, she was gonna have to get used to it.

Captains didn't stand for soldiers who didn't take orders.

The wagon was large, pulled by four mules, with a horse trailing behind—spotting the path was easy enough for anyone to find. Chloe wanted to point out the fact Gideon was doing nothing she couldn't have done, but she held her tongue. No need to rile the bear any more that morning. It was hard enough knowing her family was missing and in danger. She didn't need to start another argument with him.

Fear for Granny and the girls coated her tongue. God only knew who had taken them and why. Chloe figured the girls had been taken to be traded or sold, but why Granny? She was old, her hands didn't work good, and she was ornery. Maybe the girls were putting up such a fuss, they decided to bring along someone to watch them. For that, they needed the wagon. That made sense, even if it made her want to tear someone's arms off.

Bastards left her with hardly anything but the furniture she couldn't carry on her back. Likely everything they'd left behind would be either destroyed or long gone if—*when*—they returned to get it. Gideon had made some ingenious sacks from the linens while she had put the plates, dented coffee pot and the meager food supplies in the bag. They were currently clanking on her back as they walked.

He carried the sack he made, stuffed with two blankets and whatever else he scavenged from her family's belongings along with the tiny canteen. She didn't want to be annoyed by the fact he had gone through all their things, even if it had been necessary. Yet she was, just the same. As they walked away, she could hardly look back at what lay behind them. Her life had exploded into pieces, and what was left had been scattered around the tall grass in a field in eastern Texas.

It was almost too much to bear.

She swallowed the huge lump in her throat with effort. Chloe had been independent all her life. Being dependent on someone else, a man she had given herself to twelve hours earlier, was far outside her imagination, and she didn't know how to behave. He was cold and bossy now, barking orders at her. Good thing she was more worried about her family than his rude behavior.

Worry was something she didn't do well. She needed to find something solid to focus on, or she might start howling.

"Do you know where the next town is?" She looked ahead across the gently rolling hills and prairie and saw nothing but trees. Chloe needed to know exactly what they were doing—that would be what she hung on to, to maintain control of her emotions.

"Ahead."

Chloe counted to ten. "How long will it take us to get there?"

"Depends on how fast you walk. I can make it twenty miles in a day, but I doubt you can."

Chloe counted to ten again. "How many miles do we need to walk to get to the next town?" There, that ought to be simple enough for him to understand.

"A lot."

Her patience snapped, and she wagged her finger at his broad back. "I can keep up with any pace you set, Blackwood. Stop being such an ass. Just tell me how many miles it is and what the name of the town is."

He stopped and pivoted to look at her. "I don't know. You happy? I rode this trail more than a year ago, and things change. Most times I stay put because I have a restaurant to run. I'm following the tracks, nothing more. If we find a town, then I can wire for help. If we find the bastards that took everything, I can kill them and ride for help." He stepped close enough she could see a drop of sweat meandering down his whiskered cheek. "Anything else you need to know?"

The man was bigger than life, bossy and absolutely the most impressive thing she'd seen in her life, especially when he was mad. This wasn't the place or time to be attracted to him, but it was happening anyway. Her body was already warm from the pace Gideon had set with his long legs, and now he'd set a fire burning low and deep in her belly. Her thoughts scattered like dandelion puffs in the breeze.

She struggled to find something to say, anything to take her mind off the man. At least he had distracted her from worrying. "Do you have a weapon?"

He huffed out a breath. "No, I don't. My rifle and my pistols were hanging on the saddle. The knife I normally keep on my back when I travel was in my bedroll, since I was doing heavy lifting. All I've got are my fists and my brain."

"That's not a whole lot if we come up against the ones who stole your guns." She was only being practical. Even the strongest man could not stop a bullet with his fists alone.

"Thank you for the confidence in my ability to protect you." His tone was anything but grateful.

Chloe was insulted by the inference. "I don't need *you* to protect *me*. I've done right fine up until now. Besides, I've got a knife."

The frown on his face could have cut glass. "Why do you have a knife, and where did you hide it?" He looked her up and down, pausing briefly on her chest.

She wanted to smack him. "Why wouldn't I have a knife? I have need to protect myself too. I've got my fists, my brain and my knife. And it's in my boot, not my tits." She stuck her nose in the air and walked around him.

He cursed under his breath, but the wind carried it to her clearly. She smiled grimly and kept walking. He'd follow when he was ready.

Gideon wanted to strangle her. The little snip of a woman, barely more than a girl, was deliberately inciting his anger, didn't listen to a word he said, and she had a knife. He'd been distracted by her from the moment he realized she was a woman, and things just got worse and worse. Now they appeared to be at rock bottom.

He was at a loss as to how to speak to her, much less be on the trail with her. If only he hadn't stopped to help them, things wouldn't be so incredibly wrong. He could have been closer to Grayton, to visiting with Nate and Elisa. Hell, for that matter, he could have been home in Tanger. Instead, he was horseless, weaponless and stuck with Chloe, who happened to possess the most amazing passion he'd ever seen.

She was driving him loco, and he'd known the woman only a day. Granted, if he'd kept his hands to himself in the wagon last night, things might have been a bit less tense. But no, he hadn't kept any body part to himself.

Dammit to hell.

When he'd gotten his frustration tamped down, at least temporarily, Gideon finally started walking again. With her short legs, it didn't take him long to catch up. She wouldn't look at him, but she kept pace with him as they walked. Perversely he didn't make his stride any shorter to be considerate of the difference in size between them. It was a childish thing to do, he knew that, but he did it anyway. She had to understand he was in charge, regardless of how much it annoyed her. There had to be a chain of command or their mission would fail.

Gideon didn't like feeling out of sorts in any situation. As a captain in the army, he either controlled situations, or they controlled him. It didn't matter how difficult things were; if he could figure things out, then he would find the place where he was comfortable, in control.

The Ruskins had yanked him from that safe, organized existence into their chaos. Now he had lost his horse, his pistols and the hard-won Yankee rifle he had kept by his side since the war. It was nearly everything he valued, aside from his friends, the Devils on Horseback, named because of their bloodcurdling yells as they performed midnight raids during the war. The five of them were closer than kin, brothers in heart and soul. If he'd lost one of them, he'd be devastated. The horse and his gear, well, that would cost him a year's profit from the restaurant he co-owned just to replace them.

It took him another ten minutes to realize he was complaining, albeit to himself, about how hard it would be to lose his family, and Chloe had *lost hers.* He stopped dead in his tracks. He'd been a complete ass about the whole thing. The Ruskins didn't lure him into a situation to steal his things or make him loco. They were a family too, as odd and unusual as his own. Now they were separated through no choice of their own.

The Devils all survived the war, near starvation afterward,

and a very lean six months of running from an army captain who wanted to throw them in jail. They were all healthy, and aside from Gideon, happily married, still together in heart, if not physically. He had everything that was important to him; all he loved was safe and sound.

Not so for Chloe. Gideon felt a rush of shame at his behavior, at his petty reaction to what happened.

"Chloe."

She stopped and swiveled to face him. With a speed and agility that surprised him, she looked around and reached toward her boot, as if to retrieve her knife. Small round sweat marks stained the underarms of her hideous potato-sack dress. It was hot, and they'd been walking at least an hour, taking only sips of water, heading into the unknown without a clear direction other than the tracks. Her face was tight with worry and a wariness he recognized well. He'd seen it on his own face many times.

She was obviously exhausted, worried and hot. Gideon had ignored what she'd been going through, and for his own selfish interests, to boot.

Another item on his ever-growing list of sins.

"What's wrong?"

"I just, uh, wanted to say I'm sorry." The words almost stuck in his throat, unwilling to exit the premises without a fight.

"For what?" Her brow furrowed.

How could he explain without sounding like a complete fool?

"I should have kept a better eye on all of you, especially the girls. And I didn't get the repairs done quickly enough. I also didn't make sure the fire stayed lit last night." Gideon wanted to smack his own face for that last piece of nonsense that came out of his mouth. He hadn't even been near the fire last night.

"Do you have a flask or something? Because you sound tipsy." She shook her head. "What in tarnation are you talking about?"

Gideon approached her, stopping a few feet away. "I acted like a horse's ass, worried about my plans to visit a friend, my horse and my things. I should have been more concerned about your family."

Her mouth dropped open just a bit before she closed it, but he saw the surprise on her face. Perhaps even a bit of respect in her eyes.

"Well then, I accept your apology. Now let's get moving. They've got wheels and four-legged critters to get them where they need to be. All we've got are two feet each and a whole lot of stubbornness."

Gideon's mouth twitched with a grin. She was all full of sass. "I'd have to agree with you, surprisingly. Can we call a truce?"

"Fine by me. Let's just keep going."

This time they began their journey in earnest as partners instead of at cross-purposes. Two strangers who had been intimate, yet were still worlds apart, on a quest to find that which had been taken from them. If it hadn't been happening to him, Gideon might believe it was a book he'd read.

Chloe was more uncomfortable with him after he apologized than when they were fighting. He was being too nice, and she didn't like it. People would probably wonder if she was loco for thinking that, but she couldn't help the way she felt.

If he was annoying and bossy, she could give it right back

to him. She didn't know how to be nice to him, and she didn't want to be stuck with him. Too late for that, though, since they were bonded at a different level—not only had they been rubbing on each other in the dark, but their lives were linked because of someone's need to steal what wasn't theirs.

Chloe likely would have never met Gideon before the war, even if they had lived in the same town. She could tell by the way he talked the man had been educated well. He used words she didn't understand half the time. She wasn't about to ask him what they meant and feel even stupider than she did. Then there was the way he walked, like he could just as well be at a fancy ball with a girl wearing a fluffy yellow dress on his arm. He was from money, whether he had any now or not.

On the other side of the coin, Chloe had come from a dirt farm in Virginia with nothing more than her granny and a brother. When she was little, her mother had been killed in a flood, and then her pa gambled himself to an early death when she was fifteen. If it weren't for Granny, Chloe may have starved to death or worse. They scratched out a living trading eggs and vegetables for what they needed. Granny held on to what was left of her family's things, the furniture built by her grandfather so long ago.

Now that piece of history was left out for anyone and anything to scavenge. If the rain didn't destroy it, some settler or farmer would take it for what they could use. Chloe wouldn't blame them; her family had certainly done the same when they'd found things on the side of the trail. What was important was getting the girls and Granny back, not the eighty-year-old cabinet sitting in the tall grass miles behind them.

The decision to travel to Texas hadn't been an easy one. They had argued for weeks before Chloe relented and they started packing things into the wagon. After the war, many things were destroyed or nearly so. Moving to Texas was the only way to get a fresh start, away from the bloody battlefields around them.

Now Chloe wondered if they'd made the right choice. The journey had been rough on all of them, and now to have such a thing happen when they were close to their end goal... Why did God have to be such an ass? Why couldn't he have just given the one thing the Ruskins needed? A chance.

"You're very quiet." His voice startled her. She'd been so deep in thought, she had forgotten he was beside her.

"I'm thinking."

"I figured as much."

"You're not from Texas." She could tell by his accent that he hailed from the south somewhere.

"Neither are you." He slid her a sidelong glance.

A snort burst from her throat. "No, I'm not." She shifted the pack on her shoulder. "Where are you from?"

Gideon blew out a breath. "Georgia."

The one word held so much meaning, she could almost see it hanging in the air. It was full of longing, grief, pride and love.

"Sherman's March?"

"Yeah." This time the word was tight and sharp.

General Sherman had destroyed a great deal in his march through Georgia. She'd heard stories about the devastation. Her curiosity was almost as sharp as his answer, but she decided to hold her questions for another day. Or maybe never, but it wasn't the time now. She changed the subject instead.

"Were you a soldier? My brother was." She hadn't thought about Adam for a long time. She searched her brain for a glimpse of a memory, to bring up a vision of what he looked like.

"Yes, I was." He stared straight ahead, his face

expressionless.

"I haven't seen my brother in years, not since he marched off to war with my cousin, Tobias. Neither one of them ever returned, and they weren't on any death notices either. They just vanished into the ranks of lost soldiers." She closed her eyes and finally was able to picture them smiling as they shined the buttons on the coats Granny had made for them. They were barely eighteen, not even men yet. Boys with big ideas and more gumption than they could hold.

"I'm sorry."

She shrugged. "Nothing for you to be sorry for. The war changed plenty of folks' lives."

"Truer words were never spoken." Gideon glanced up at the sky. "With this sun beating down on us, the water won't last long. I can turn that leather bag I found into a carrying bag and find another source of water."

He apparently didn't want to talk about the war anymore, which was fine with her. She'd seen plenty from the sidelines, considering the fighting was almost on her farm. Blood and violence abounded for years, becoming a part of her life she wanted desperately to forget.

They split up, walking twenty feet apart, looking and listening for a water source. She tried not to pay attention to him as she searched for water, but she caught herself watching his big frame in motion. For a large man, he was incredibly stealthy, his feet barely making a sound. He was a tracker, and she had to trust that he knew what he was doing. Chloe managed to push aside her obsession with Gideon and focus on her search.

"Here. There's a small pond," he called from a distance away.

She made her way through the trees to Gideon. He knelt by

the edge of the pond, sniffing a handful of water. He took a small sip, then a larger one.

"Is it good water?"

"It isn't the best, but it's drinkable." He tossed her the leather pouch. "Clean that as best you can, and let's see if we can make a waterskin out of it."

She caught the pouch and touched the soft leather. It had been her grandpappy's tobacco pouch, stained by years of the leaf he'd tucked inside it. It could hold the water to keep her alive, which Granny would approve of. With a bit of wistfulness completely unlike her, she opened the pouch.

The sweet smell of tobacco wafted toward her, invoking memories she'd locked away, of good times with her grandparents and her brother, of a life she'd lost. She pressed her fist into her chest and tried to will away the ache that blossomed.

"Stop daydreaming and get moving. Every minute we stay here is a minute we lose." Gideon's voice was gruff and, no surprise, commanding. He was already filling the tiny canteen up again.

Instead of yelling, Chloe tossed the pouch at him and walked away without a word. It was too much to handle, too much loss to bear all at once. She missed those simple times on the farm, the normalness of a predictable life. Now she was stuck in the middle of nowhere with a stranger, more than a thousand miles from home.

Gideon was behind her in seconds. "What's wrong now, Chloe?"

Chloe threw her hands in the air. "Everything. I've lost my family piece by piece until there's nothing left but the pouch in your hand." She snatched it from him and shook it. "This little pouch right here."

He nodded, understanding in his eyes. "Then we'll find something else to carry water in."

Chloe slipped the pouch into her bag for safekeeping. Pitiful as it was, the pouch truly was all she had left, other than a couple blankets and pots and pans.

They drank their fill of water and started walking again, all conversation tucked away. The tension between them had dissipated. The tobacco pouch had established a hesitant truce for which Chloe was grateful. Theirs had been a strange relationship that only got odder as the hours passed.

The tracks in the road gave her something solid to hold on to. Two of the mules had nicks in their shoes, and their progress was easily marked. The one thing she was glad of was having someone to travel with, even if he was the last person she expected to be with when she woke up yesterday.

Life wasn't done throwing mountains in her path yet.

Chapter Four

After plodding along for three hours, Gideon regretted giving her back the pouch. The water in the tiny canteen was gone, and they hadn't found much more than puddles long since turned to mud. He was thirsty, tired and knew they'd need to find water soon, or they would have to stop for the day.

It was early afternoon, and the late spring heat permeated the air. His shirt stuck to his back beneath the pack he wore. Trickles of sweat meandered down his cheeks and neck. He would pay good money for a bucket full of well water to dunk his head into, hell, to douse his whole body with.

Maybe they'd get lucky and find something around the next copse of trees. Of course, as a soldier, he didn't believe in luck. He had to make his own, which meant they might have to change their plan.

Chloe looked as bad as he felt. Her hair was hanging in strings, her dress was in even worse shape than before and her expression was pinched. They needed water in the worst way. Much as she might not like it, he'd have to break off tracking the wagon.

"We need to find fresh water, or neither one of us is going to be any good." He took off his hat, almost moaning as the small breeze caressed his sweat-soaked brow.

"There will be some along the way. This trail is well used,

and folks ain't gonna use it if they can't find water." She plodded along at a steady pace without turning in his direction.

Gideon silently agreed with her. "That might be so, but I've seen a couple of dry creek beds along the way. It's also possible this trail hasn't been used in a while because the water dried up."

"It doesn't matter if it did. We can keep going without it."

"No, we can't." He took hold of her arm to stop her. "You look like you're about to perish."

Her lip curled. "You sure do know how to flatter a lady."

"I'm sure I don't look much better." He didn't have time to be thinking about her delicate sensibilities or whether his words offended her. It was time to make command decisions. "If we both get too weak to go on or too weak to fight for them, then we've defeated ourselves before we even got started."

Chloe pulled out of his grasp. "I ain't losing their trail because you're thirsty."

Gideon swallowed his angry retort before he spoke. "It's hot, we're sweating and we haven't had a drink in hours. That means all the water we have in our bodies is leaving without putting more in. I've seen men drop dead after marching for days without fresh water." He leaned in close and noticed just how long her lashes were. She was such a damn distraction. "The tracks should be easy to pick up again, but we are going to have to stop to find water. We also need to find something else to carry it in or make something."

He didn't mention the tobacco pouch and wasn't going to. It was important to her, and he respected that. However he wasn't about to let her kill herself because she didn't want to listen to what he had to say.

"I ain't stopping. You go ahead and find yourself a drink, but I'm moving on." She walked on, heedless of the fact it was completely illogical, not to mention maddening.

"Chloe." He started after her, then stopped and listened. The sound of wagon wheels echoed faintly in the afternoon air. He snatched her up by the waist, covering her mouth with one hand so she couldn't scream, and dove into the brush.

The woman was like a wildcat in his arms, bucking and twisting, even biting his hand. He leaned down and whispered harshly in her ear, "Shut up and be still. There's a wagon coming."

She quieted, but the daggers shooting from her eyes got sharper.

"You ready to be good?" He wasn't playing games with her, but damned if he didn't have to treat her like a little kid.

She was anything but a little kid though. Her breasts pushed into his arm and stomach, and her body, honed by years of work, tucked into his like a key in a lock. Stupid dick noticed it all. It twitched against her hip, and her eyes opened wide, then narrowed again.

Gideon let her loose, momentarily flummoxed by his reaction to this spritely creature. She was a stranger, a woman he'd bedded because she had crawled in beside him offering herself. Chloe Ruskin meant nothing to him, yet his body disagreed. She was definitely more than nothing, perhaps bordering on something.

"You keep that stick in your pants, mister." She scrambled a few feet away. "I ain't got the time to please your inclinations right now."

If they weren't in such dire straits, he might have laughed at the notion he had to keep his "inclinations" to himself. It was absurd to consider that he would force himself on a woman, much less put their lives at risk to do so. Women didn't quite understand how a man's dick did the most outrageous things, whether or not he wanted it to. Sometimes it took control, however short-lived, until Gideon took it back, with force, if necessary.

"Take off your pack and leave it here until we know who is in the wagon. As for my inclinations, I don't have the time or the desire to do anything to you right now." He kept his voice barely audible. "Now shut up and listen."

He was surprised to see something like hurt pass across her features as she turned away from him. There was no way she could be insulted because he wasn't going to fuck her in the woods. For God's sake, they were potentially waiting for the men who kidnapped her family and stole his horse. The very idea she'd been hurt was ridiculous. His words couldn't hurt the thick-skinned Chloe.

She wanted to punch him. He'd been rude, bossy and insulting, not to mention the fact he'd manhandled her. For pity's sake, the man had carried her like a sack of potatoes. Then when his cock had pushed against her, he'd acted annoyed. Gideon Blackwood was a mean son of a bitch, and she'd do best to forget ever having given him her virginity.

Chloe took a deep, slow breath and focused. If the wagon they heard was hers, she would need her wits about her, not stuck in a rut thinking about a stranger. She pulled the knife from her boot, and he found a sturdy branch to use as a club. Pitiful weapons to be sure, but Gideon and Chloe also had the element of surprise.

She gripped the handle so hard her knuckles popped. Blood whooshed through her veins, pumping her full of energy until she almost vibrated. Her legs tensed as the sounds grew closer, then closer still. The wagon was only about fifteen feet away. Her heart thumped hard, yet she retained her control, ready to do battle with those who would harm her family.

Gideon turned and pointed at her, then to her right. He pointed at himself, then to his left. She didn't know exactly what he meant but surmised he was telling her to take the back of the wagon while he would go to the front. Chloe nodded and crept closer to the opening in the bushes as silently as she could. When she glanced back, she was surprised to see he was ten feet from her and nearly at the edge of the trail. For a big man, he moved like a shadow.

He stopped with a fist in the air, and she froze in place. Her breath came in short bursts as adrenaline surged through her. This wasn't the first time Chloe had done something potentially dangerous. It was exciting to be doing something, to be fighting for what was hers, to take a stand and hold firm. Perhaps if she'd been a man, Chloe would have fought in the war with the same kind of excitement mixed with fear. She watched and waited until he glanced her way and, with a nod, jumped out of the brush.

She ran to the back of the wagon and skidded to a stop. This was not her family's wagon. It belonged to a peddler or something like that, covered with bits and pieces of things for sale. As she turned to find Gideon, a bloodcurdling cry split the air and a shiver raced down her spine. Chloe raced around to the front of the wagon to find Gideon with his hands up and a woman pointing a shotgun at him.

Ironically familiar sight.

"I shall not let ye steal my soul, ye devil!" The woman was dressed in a drab gray dress with a poke bonnet that had seen better days. She held the weapon with ease, telling Chloe she could easily kill Gideon if desired.

"I said I was sorry, ma'am. I thought you were someone else." He spotted Chloe and gestured with his head. "There is my, ah, wife. She can tell you I meant no harm to you."

The word wife made Chloe lose her balance for a second, but she kept on walking, strangely pleased to have the man at her mercy again. It was an inappropriate moment to be having such thoughts, but they persisted anyway. Things had been topsy-turvy since she'd lowered her own pistol the day before. Impossible to think it had been just over one day, but time didn't lie.

The stranger turned to look at Chloe but kept her gun firmly pointed at Gideon.

"This your man here?"

Chloe's gaze met Gideon's, and she saw so much in that split second, it startled her. Partly because she wanted to have someone to call her man, and because she saw the same kind of longing in his eyes.

"Ah, yes, ma'am. This here is Gideon." Chloe stumbled over her words just as much as she'd done with her feet moments earlier. Mr. Blackwood made her awkward inside and out.

"You best drop that knife, girlie, and come on over to your Gideon."

The older woman's voice was hard as granite. Chloe wasn't taking any chances, so she scurried over to his side, hiding the knife in the folds of her skirt.

"Don't think I don't see that knife. Unless you want to be picking up your man's brain offa the ground, you'd better throw it to me, so's you can't reach it." The woman knew how to handle a weapon. She threw rope at them while keeping her bead on Chloe and Gideon.

"Tie one of his hands to one of yours, and make sure it's tight."

"What? Why?"

"'Cause I said so, that's why. I ain't letting two strangers get hold of all my treasures. I don't trust nobody. Until that big man is tied up, this gun is pointed at his head."

Chloe bent down to pick up the rope, frantically trying to devise a way out of actually tying them up, but he stopped her thoughts with a harsh whisper.

"Just do it. We have nothing to steal but the packs we left in the bushes." He held out his hands. "If she wants a battered tin pot, she can have it."

Chloe wanted to protest but knew he was right. If the woman had a hankering for what they had, she could take it. After all, everyone seemed to be helping themselves to the Ruskin family's belongings. Why not let her join in? Bitter thoughts raced around as she tied the rope around his wrist with a yank.

"Easy, little one. She said tight, not cut off his hand." Gideon sounded as frustrated as she was.

"Sorry." She loosened the knots a bit so his hand wasn't turning purple anymore.

"Hurry up there, girlie. I ain't got all day. Tie your hand to his." The stranger watched closely as Chloe finished off the knot, leaving another six feet of rope dangling.

What if the woman made them walk behind the wagon tied like a dog?

Chloe wanted to pick up her knife and cut the rope, but again Gideon stopped her.

"We'll get free. Don't worry. I've escaped from knots tied by tougher folks than you." He squeezed her hand.

Chloe turned to their captor. "Now what?"

"Now put your other hand behind your back and wait." The woman climbed down from the wagon. As she moved closer, the smell hit first. It was worse than anything she'd ever encountered before, ten times worse. Obviously this strange peddler woman hadn't bathed in a very long time, perhaps even a year. The rancidness of her body odor made Chloe's eyes water. Gideon coughed, then cursed under his breath. The woman tied their other hands with the rope. She pushed it against Chloe's mouth. "Now tighten it with your teeth."

Chloe bit down on the filthy rope. It tasted of dirt and rotten potatoes. Frustration roared through her, and she wanted to spit at the stranger.

What else could go wrong?

Gideon gritted his teeth and barely avoided biting at the woman who had taken them captive. She was tall, much bigger than Chloe, and that shotgun had looked far too comfortable in her hands. If only the stranger had let them go about their business. But no, God had other plans, more frustration and obstacles, to throw in Gideon's path.

As the woman came closer, the stench from her unwashed body made his gorge rise. She obviously didn't take to soap and water, but she must not be able to actually smell, either. Chloe grunted and hissed as the stranger tightened the knots around her hands. Now he and Chloe were tied together, with enough rope to turn around and be chest to chest.

Clever. This way neither of them could get very far without the other, and there was such a huge difference between Gideon's height and Chloe's, he'd have to somehow carry her to run. The damn hag knew what she was doing.

"Now you can tell me what you're doing threatening good folks like me and waving a knife around." She picked up Chloe's knife, which promptly disappeared into the voluminous folds of the woman's gray skirt.

"We're looking for my kin." Chloe sounded like she was holding her nose—he didn't blame her one bit. His eyes were watering enough it might appear as if he were crying. "Somebody took my little sisters and granny, along with the wagon and mules."

"And my horse."

"Oh yeah, and his horse, uh, Deuce." Chloe was quick, he'd give her that. His horse was not named Deuce, but he wasn't about to point that out.

The woman looked at them dubiously, her dark eyes hidden beneath the ratty hat she wore. "You are chasing these folks who took everything with nothing but a knife? You expect me to believe that pile of horse shit?"

Chloe's entire body stiffened, and he knew she'd open her mouth and make things worse. As it always was in his everyday life, it fell to Gideon to be the peacemaker.

"It's true whether or not you believe it. The girls are five, with light blonde hair and blue eyes. Hazel and Martha are a passel of trouble sometimes, but they're good girls." He watched the strange woman, ignoring Chloe's elbow as it jammed into his side. "We were trying to catch up to them on foot because that's all we've got right now. Our feet and a determination to take back what was stolen from us."

The silence was broken only by the chattering of squirrels and a few birds calling to their mates. The woman stared at both of them while keeping her grip on the shotgun. If she didn't believe them, she could leave Chloe and Gideon tied up on the side of the trail, or worse.

"Please, ma'am, we just want to be on our way. You can keep the knife."

"That's my knife." Chloe wasn't giving an inch.

"Not now, Chloe," he snapped.

"It's about all I have left from my brother. He gave it to me before he went to war."

"It's just a thing. You have your memories."

"Says you. I don't want to lose the only thing I have left of him."

"That's enough, Chloe." Gideon turned until they were nose to nose. "Let her have the knife. It's not worth your life."

Chloe's green eyes sparked like sun on a lake. She was obviously mad, but it wasn't at him, rather at their situation. He understood that, but she had to stop and recognize hanging on to something for sentimental reasons was going to get her a one-way ticket to a hole in the ground.

The woman broke her silence. "You surely sound married, but there ain't no ring on her finger."

"Had to sell it to leave Georgia." The lie rolled off his tongue too easily. "We wanted to start fresh in Texas and had no money to get here. It doesn't mean we're not married, just that we don't need a ring to feel married."

Thankfully Chloe stopped poking him with her sharp elbow.

"That's right romantic of you, but I don't believe it." The old woman gestured with the shotgun. "Now get up in the seat of the wagon. I don't care how you get up there, just do it."

Gideon wanted to shout at the heavens at the stupidity of the request, but he didn't. Chloe didn't have the sense to do the same.

"Where do you think we're going to go?" Chloe snapped. "I swear to all that's holy, if you don't let us go right now, you will live to regret it. We have to follow that trail, or we're going to lose it."

She was right, of course, and Gideon didn't want to

chastise her for caring about her family or what happened to them. This stranger had put them at risk because of her distrust and inhospitable way of treating people. He wanted his horse back and his things, but most of all, he wanted to get Chloe's family back safely. It was a promise he'd made to her whether or not he actually said the words.

"Get a move on. Get up in that seat before I show you how sharp your woman's knife is." The woman jammed the shotgun into his side. "Which way they headed?"

"North. We were tracking them when we heard a wagon." Gideon sucked in a breath at how damn hard she shoved that gun in his back. "We told you we thought you were them, which is why we were in the brush waiting."

The woman tutted. "Lies, lies, lies."

Gideon started to climb into the wagon without the use of his hands, not an easy task. He leaned forward to prevent himself from falling on Chloe, but the seat dug into his chest as he tried to climb up higher.

"I can't get up there without using my hands." Gideon puffed out a breath.

"Figure it out, soldier boy. I ain't letting the two of you out of my sight." The woman was either younger than she appeared or fast as lightning. She was already in the wagon, pointing the gun at his face. He had only a second to wonder why she called him soldier boy.

Chloe growled from behind him. She had scaled the wagon enough to be almost on top of him. "Move it, Blackwood." She bent toward him and used her shoulders to push him just enough to get up on the seat, then scrambled up beside him.

They both breathed heavily as their gazes met. Fury and fear warred in her eyes, and he understood she needed him to find a way to follow her family, no matter what.

"How am I going to drive the wagon if my hands are tied? You've got a pair of horses here. I need to be able to hold the traces, or we'll end up dead in a ditch."

"Just set still a moment and I'll tell you how."

Something tugged at his foot. When he glanced down, he saw the woman under the seat tying their feet together. His left foot was now attached to Chloe's right.

"What the hell are you doing?"

"I'm going to loose one of your hands and one of hers. You can't get far tied together, and you'll have to figure out a way to drive the wagon with each other." She cackled as she made quick work of loosing the knot on his right and Chloe's left hands. This was the knot the woman had tied herself, obviously a slipknot she'd expected to undo. He was going to grab the woman, but she had the shotgun firmly situated at the base of his back. If his attempt failed, she could literally cut him in two.

With a slam of the shotgun barrel on his spine, she sat back. He couldn't see her without turning around. Chloe's left hand was a fist on her leg. The knuckles were white, nearly bloodless.

"Don't lose them, Gideon." Her whisper was harsh but full of emotion.

"I won't." He picked up the traces and handed her half. "I promise."

They started off in the opposite direction they had been headed. It would mean another delay in finding the Ruskins' wagon. He had to find a way to turn around or risk losing the trail completely.

As the afternoon wore on, the tension grew tighter with each passing minute. Chloe had never experienced such red-hot rage for someone, not even the damn Yankee bastard who'd stolen their last sack of corn when they'd been starving. This woman had destroyed the likelihood of tracking her family.

Chloe didn't cry much, but the possibility she would never see Granny or the girls again brought tears to her eyes. She turned her head and watched the trees go by until she had willed the tears away. The wagon trudged on with the two of them driving the team of sorry-looking nags. To her surprise, Gideon's right-hand method complemented her left, and they drove together with ease. Of course it required her to be hip to hip with him, their tied hands resting on his knee. His leg was exceptionally strong and hard—there wasn't much about Gideon Blackwood that was soft.

His face seemed to be set in granite now, and she could see he was controlling his anger through iron will. While she gritted her teeth and cursed every two minutes, he stared straight ahead, a rock beside her on the wagon seat.

"What are we going to do?" she whispered harshly.

"I'm thinking," was his cryptic response.

"Think faster."

"You two better stop jawin' up there. I ain't gonna let you get away from me until I know exactly what you was doing at my wagon." The hideous woman leaned forward, unleashing a fresh waft of rancid body odor.

"Fine, we won't talk, just move back where you were." Chloe breathed through her mouth to avoid the stench.

"Why? You conspirin' to do somethin'?" She leaned even closer, and Chloe's eyes began to water for a different reason.

"No, because you smell like an outhouse that ain't been cleaned in two years," Chloe snapped.

"Well, la-di-da, ain't you the fine lady? I don't like bathing, but that don't mean nothin'. I'm smart and got this here wagon full of goods to sell to settlers." The woman cackled again. "You two ain't got nothin' but an old knife and the clothes on your back." She pressed the barrel of the shotgun into Chloe's neck. "Now who's a better person?"

Chloe didn't answer, because she enjoyed having her head attached to her body. The peddler woman was completely loco. She would probably shoot them and leave their bodies by the side of the road for the vultures to pick at. Not a chance Chloe would let that happen.

Two excruciating hours passed before they stopped. Chloe had a feeling the woman had to relieve herself, and unfortunately, so did she. They all climbed down out of the wagon, with Gideon having the hardest time since they were now tied together at the ankle and wrist.

If it had been a different day, a different situation, Chloe might have laughed at the sight of him inching down like an old man. The peddler woman got annoyed with him and poked him in the back.

"Hurry up there, soldier boy. I ain't got all day."

He stopped and turned to look at her. "Why do you call me that?"

Her gap-toothed grin was feral. "Ain't that what you are? A soldier boy? I could see it in your eyes and the way you move. Cain't hide that from Annie. Them soldiers are usually desperate. They trade me favors for things." She leaned in closer to Gideon, and Chloe saw beneath the dirt and grime. The woman was barely older than she was! Then she pressed her breasts into Gideon's arm.

Chloe wanted to tear that bitch to pieces.

"I am not that desperate." He started climbing down again.

His barb, however, hit its mark. The woman snarled and

grabbed for Gideon. It was Chloe's opportunity.

In a blink, she twisted away as far as she could, then kicked out with all her might. A crack resounded when her boot connected solidly with the woman's arm. The gun flipped until it was pointing up.

Gideon moved like lightning. Chloe couldn't even focus on him—he was a blur. When it was over, he held the gun, she was safe at his side, and their captor lay on the ground screeching and clutching her arm.

"I knew you was a soldier boy the second I laid eyes on you. That bitch of yours broke my arm."

"Good. You deserve it for kidnapping us and forcing us to tie each other up." He pressed the gun against her head. "Now tell me why."

"I don't know what you mean."

Gideon pulled the hammer back. "Oh, I think you do. How much did they pay you to waylay us?"

Chloe's mouth dropped open. "What the hell are you talking about?"

He pointed at the peddler. "I think whoever took the girls and Granny paid her to stop us from following. How much was it? Or did they get between your legs too?"

The woman snorted. "I ain't gonna admit to nothing."

Gideon leaned down to whisper to Chloe. "Get our hands untied, then our feet."

She wanted to muster up some annoyance at him for bossing her around, but she found herself glad he'd been there. Life had turned itself inside out and upside down. She was comforted by his smarts and his presence. What if Gideon hadn't been there when everything had gone horribly wrong? It was a bit like eating crow, but Chloe admitted to herself that she needed him.

Chloe untied them in a flash, glad of her calloused fingers against the rough rope. She had to use her teeth to get their hands untied. Other than his cheek twitching, Gideon showed no reaction to having her mouth on his wrists.

"Now tie her up."

With something like vengeful glee, she did as he bade. The stench was even worse close up, and the crazy woman tried to bite her a few times. She even howled as the rope tightened around the injured arm. Chloe wondered if she was hurt at all, based on how many times the woman bared her teeth and snarled like an animal caught in a trap.

"Now, we're going to do you the courtesy of leaving you by the side of the trail while we take your wagon and head back the way we came. If you're lucky, we won't send the law after you for at least a day." Gideon squatted down and stared at her eye to eye. "I will make you a promise. If I ever see you again, I won't hesitate to kill you. Your actions may have caused harm to two innocent little girls and their grandmother, not to mention what you've done to my wife. I don't forgive, and I never forget."

Chloe had seen him angry, annoyed, amused and focused, but she wasn't prepared for the coldness in his eyes. They were sharp enough to cut glass, even sent a shiver up her spine. He showed the world a mostly patient, helpful gentleman, but inside him was a controlled animal waiting to go to battle. This must be what the woman saw—the soldier boy beneath the curly brown hair and pretty blue eyes.

The peddler woman spit at him. "Big words, especially when I'm tied up."

"I could dig a hole for you instead."

The woman's breath caught. His threat was real enough to

make Chloe more than glad he was on her side.

"Bastard."

"No, my parents were actually married." Gideon poked her with the gun. "Now walk toward the woods."

Her eyes widened, and she glanced at Chloe as if expecting an intervention. Slim chance of that happening.

"You cain't take my wagon."

"Oh yes I can and I will. We need something with wheels to catch the sons of bitches we're chasing." Gideon rose like an avenging angel, his eyes shooting sparks of fury. "Now *move*."

His tone didn't leave a smidge of room for arguing. Neither did the way he held the gun, with a sureness that told her he had spent a good deal of time in his life with a weapon. Chloe scrambled out of the way and watched as the woman shuffled toward the woods, her expression promising retribution. It didn't matter though—they would never see her again, and she was certain Gideon would hold to his promise. If they happened to cross paths with the woman, he would kill her.

"Get in the wagon, Chloe."

Again, she obeyed without a peep. Later on she'd have to speak to him about bossing her around so much. She got herself settled on the seat and held the reins. Gideon watched the woman until she was at least fifty yards away, then glanced up at Chloe. His smile was not a happy one.

"Now let's get this thing turned around so we can find your family."

Chloe wanted to whoop and crow like a rooster, but she kept that locked away for now. He was focused on the right task—finding her family. He took hold of the lead horse and led him around in a circle until they were pointing back the way they came. Then he climbed on the side and hung on as the wagon began to move. He kept the shotgun pointed at their kidnapper, never moving from his post until they were long out of sight.

Chapter Five

Gideon was furious. Not only had he allowed the stranger to keep them tied up and captive for a good portion of the day, but Chloe had changed their circumstances instead of him. It was his job to be the one doing the rescuing and planning, not hers. Yet he had hesitated to do what needed to be done because he was afraid she would get hurt.

Now the idea made him nearly snort. She was not only fearless, she was smart and quick as hell. They'd been tied together, yet she'd managed to injure the peddler woman, maintain her balance and give him the opportunity to disarm their enemy. It was damn embarrassing, frustrating and impressive.

After they were far enough away to be safe for now, he climbed up into the wagon and sat beside Chloe. He set the shotgun in front of them on the floor and held out his hands. She just raised one brow.

"What makes you think I'm gonna let you drive?"

Gideon gritted his teeth. "Because I'm the man here."

"I'd say we're equal partners, Blackwood. We were a team back there, and you're gonna have to let me hold the reins now and again."

It made sense, of course. Logic over emotion and all that, but he didn't give a shit about logic. He just wanted to feel as if he was in control, even if he wasn't.

"For right now, just hand it over."

She must have seen something in his expression, because she sighed dramatically and gave him the reins. Gideon wondered if she were humoring him but didn't want to take that thought any further. Right now he would focus on the trail ahead of them and getting back to where they had been as soon as possible. Unfortunately, the team was old and plodded along slower than he thought possible. They would need some fresh blood to pull this wagon, or they would never catch the people they chased.

They moved along at a snail's pace, the sound of the merchandise in the wagon behind them clanking and banging together as the wheels hit dips in the trail. It was a strange kind of music—one he did not want to get used to hearing. He planned on getting rid of the wagon as soon as they found the Ruskins. For now he would endure it and its hideous stench.

"Do you think we can find our way back to the packs we left behind?" Chloe's voice was surprisingly calm.

"Maybe, but with all the shit in this wagon, we don't need any supplies."

She murmured something he didn't quite catch. Five minutes later, she apparently could not control her tongue any longer. "I want that pack back. It's likely all we have left of our things, and I don't want to show up on my aunt's doorstep with nothing but dirty drawers and bugs in my hair."

"This is the same trail we followed west. If we keep going, we'll end up where we were this afternoon." He could almost feel her grinning at him. "But there's no guarantee we'll find the exact spot, and we can't afford to be poking around in the woods."

She nodded. "I understand that, and I would probably say

the same thing. But in this case, I can find the spot."

"How is that possible? It was a bunch of trees with no distinguishing landmarks." Gideon thought maybe she was trying to trick him into searching for the packs. There was no chance she could find a bush in the middle of the thick woods they had left them in.

"Distinguishing landmarks? You sure do talk fancy." She shook her head. "I cut an X in the tree bark."

"You did what?"

"You heard me. I marked the tree with my knife when you was getting captured." Chloe sounded so damn smug, his annoyance notched up further.

He told himself not to react, to let her have her moment of triumph. Overall, Gideon was the better soldier, even if she'd been the one who freed them from their captivity. She was a young woman, cocky and sure of herself. There was no reason for him to get riled up.

But damned if he didn't.

Before he even realized what he was doing, Gideon dropped the reins and yanked her close to him for a bruising kiss. It was a clashing of lips, teeth and tongue, different from their midnight sex. This was primal, elemental and overwhelming. Perhaps it was because they had faced danger together and escaped. He knew he was lying to himself, but thinking wasn't an option at the moment.

In fact, he could hardly breathe.

The salty taste of her lips gave way to the sweetness of her mouth. The hot, wet recesses beckoned him until he was so deep he couldn't distinguish where she ended and he began. His dick hardened in an instant, pressing against his trousers, eager to find release with Chloe. To his shock, her hand started pulling on the buttons to free him. He was about to stop her when she spoke.

"Please, I need. Now." It was a fractured thought but one he understood.

He yanked at the offending buttons until the evening air hit his overheated skin. Her hand surrounded him, and he groaned into her mouth. Thank God she wore drawers with a slit. The ugly dress bunched around her hips. Chloe straddled him, never breaking the kiss, and soon he was poised at her entrance, which was already wet with arousal.

It was wrong, it was foolhardy, it was loco. He couldn't stop if someone put a gun to his head.

Gideon had never been as aroused or as hard as he was at that moment. She sank onto his length, inch by inch, her tightness surrounding him, embracing him. He gripped the seat beside him until the wood almost splintered under his fingers. It was only through sheer force of will he did not come in the first five seconds. She was perfectly made for him, as if someone had engineered her tiny body to accept, welcome, enclose his.

"Ohhhhh," she breathed against his lips. "It's even better than last night."

Damn straight it was. Gideon guided her up and down a few times, and then she took control again. Her pace increased quickly until all he could do was hang on to her hips and try not to find his release too soon. Blood raced around inside him until his heartbeat became the only thing he heard.

The sounds of the forest around them ceased, and the air became still. The world held its breath as Gideon and Chloe moved together as one being in an ancient rhythm, hearts thumping, breath catching. Sliding against one another, their moans echoing softly into the dense forest.

Her pussy began to twitch, and he knew her release was imminent. He surrendered control and let himself fly with her.

Her soft, keening cry reached his ears as he shouted. The pleasure coursed through him with the force of a mule kick, stealing his breath and stopping his heart, until stars exploded behind his eyes. His fingers dug into her hips as her fingers did the same to his shoulders.

It was the most powerful orgasm of his life.

Every inch of his body trembled with the force of their joining. She rested her forehead against his, her breath mingling with his choppy gusts.

"I didn't know." Her voice was huskier than normal.

"Know what?" His sounded like rusty metal.

She sat up and looked into his eyes. "What it felt like to have your man call your name like that."

Gideon's throat closed up as he studied her guileless green eyes. It was true whether or not he wanted to accept it. He had shouted her name when he came, something he'd never done in his life. Not once.

That's when he knew he was in trouble.

Chloe hoped he couldn't tell she was trembling. The movement of the wagon likely hid the fact she could not stop shaking. The first time she'd been with Gideon, it had been dark and mostly about feeling new things. This was at sunset, on a wagon seat, and she'd ridden him like he was a horse.

What made her off-kilter, though, was when he had said her name. Granny hadn't told her much about what men did or what happened to them during sex. Chloe figured out on her own that men made noises when they found their pleasure. He called her name this time. *Her* name. What did it mean? She wished Granny were there to ask.

Instead she sat next to him and tried to look as though

nothing was wrong. The truth was far from that though—everything was wrong. There was no use getting riled up when there wasn't a thing she could do to change what had happened the last two days. Done was done.

"Where did you mark them?"

She started at the sound of his voice, slid sideways and got a few splinters in her behind. "Jesus Christmas!" She took a deep breath and tried to stop acting like a fool. "Mark what?"

He pursed his lips and appeared to be controlling his temper. She knew personally those lips were much softer than they appeared.

Stop thinking about his dang lips.

"The trees, Chloe. You said you had marked them with your knife."

"On the bark."

His eyes narrowed. "I realize it's on the bark. What I'm asking is did you mark them high, in the middle, on the roots?"

Chloe wished she were anywhere but that very spot. Vibrations echoed between her legs, his seed was on her thighs, and he was treating her like she was an idiot. Instead of letting her temper and her pride overtake her again, she turned away from him. If she wasn't looking at him, perhaps she could regain some semblance of self-control.

"I made an X at eye level." She wasn't surprised to hear her voice had grown huskier. Emotions were not something she welcomed or relished, and they were surrounding her at the moment.

"Low on the tree."

She opened her mouth to repeat *eye level* but realized the marks were low on the tree, comparatively speaking, that was. Her short stature was always a source of annoyance, especially around men who were as big as trees.

"Yep, I reckon you're right." The words were pulled from her throat.

"Start looking, then. It's almost too dark to see, and I'm pretty sure we're near where we started with the peddler." He gave orders, again, and held the reins so nonchalantly she wanted to smack him. Wasn't he as affected as she was by what they had just done? If not, then why?

She had no one to ask and no answers to the million questions in her mind. She focused on what she could do—find the trees she'd scored. As the minutes passed, she grew worried they wouldn't find the packs in the dark, much less Granny and the girls. She must have been fidgeting on the seat.

"Is something biting you?"

She glanced at him. "Why?"

"You're dancing over there like an army of ants is biting at you." His scowl made his eyebrows touch like two caterpillars kissing.

She ignored him. After all, she could fidget if she wanted to. He was not her real husband, and he had no say in what she did. Maybe annoying him would become a game until, well, until they lost control again. That couldn't, *shouldn't*, happen another time. It didn't stop her traitorous body from warming to the idea. Was she turning into a wanton? Granny didn't warn her about that. In fact, Granny didn't warn her about a lot of things.

Like how her skin tingled at his touch, or how she throbbed before, during and after joining with him, or how his lips had blazed a trail of fire across her. Now she was beginning to fidget, and it wasn't because of ants.

"More ants?"

She wanted to smack him. "If you have to know, I'm just worried is all."

Liar.

"Me too." He tried again in vain to get the horses to move a bit faster. They did not respond to his call or the traces lightly smacking their rumps. "I can't make these nags into stallions no matter how hard I try. We'll just have to keep moving and hope we find something."

That something turned out to be the trees she had scored. The night air was cooling things off, but anxiety and stress made sweat trickle down her back as she squinted at the forest. At first she thought she was seeing things because she wanted so badly to find the marks. Then she grabbed his arm, surprised again by how it felt to touch such a muscular man. She shook off the feeling.

"Stop the wagon. I think I see something."

Before he could even react, she jumped out and ran toward the trees. She nearly wept when she saw the X she had swiped with her knife hours earlier. Her finger traced the letter as she worked at swallowing the lump in her throat. They were back on track, back to where their detour started, and now they could pick up the trail of the Ruskin wagon.

The sound of clanking drew her attention, and she saw Gideon had retrieved their packs already. He was staring into the back of the peddler's wagon and shaking his head. Finally more in control of her runaway emotions, Chloe stepped over to where he stood.

"What's wrong?"

"What's right?" He gestured to the wagon. "There is so much junk in here I can't even figure out what most of this stuff is." He pushed aside a pile of what appeared to be burlap sacks to set down their homemade packs. "I wouldn't put these any farther in or we'll never see them again."

Gideon climbed in, and she squawked in protest. "What are you doing now?"

"Looking for more weapons."

"Oh." Made sense to her and she wondered why she hadn't thought of it. "Can I help?"

"I don't think there's room in here for me to change my mind, much less room for a sprite like you."

She narrowed her eyes. "That just means I can move around easier in there, and faster too. Now if you get out, I can get in and search before it's completely dark."

Gideon wasn't happy about her logic, but he must have agreed with it, because he climbed down out of the wagon. He obviously didn't like being wrong or letting her be correct. The thought made her want to smile, but the time just wasn't right for that. She dug around, encountering more smells, sights and surprises than she cared to. Her hands were sticky and dirty by the time she had found six knives, a rusty pistol and a shotgun. She handed each one to Gideon as she located them.

"Any ammunition for these?"

She felt a little foolish not looking for the shells and bullets, but she didn't want him to know that. "I'm looking for them now."

Chloe had to hold her breath a few times as she dug through the accumulation of shit the old woman had packed in the wagon. There didn't appear to be any rhyme or reason to her organization of things, so every nook and cranny had to be searched. The good news was Chloe did find ammunition, even some for guns they hadn't found.

As she handed the boxes to Gideon, she couldn't help but give him a triumphant smile. "I found more than what we need."

He smiled in return, and Chloe's world tilted a bit sideways. For all the times she'd seen an expression on his face, she'd never seen a true smile. It transformed him into the most handsome man she had ever laid eyes on. The man's looks were positively lethal.

"What's wrong?" His smile turned upside down, breaking the spell.

"Nothing that some fresh air won't cure. There's some powerful stink in here."

He held out his hands to help her down, and she was going to tell him no, she could get down by herself. After all, hadn't he seen her leap from the moving wagon earlier? However, she didn't have time to tell him a thing. He grabbed her by the waist and plucked her from the wagon as if she weighed no more than a feather.

"Jesus, you are a little bit of a thing, aren't you?" His voice had dropped low, his tone making a shiver dance across her skin.

"Big enough." She couldn't help but remember what had happened between them on the wagon seat. How it felt to have him deep inside her again. Her pussy throbbed once, and she stepped away from him, somewhat afraid of her reaction to his nearness.

"Fast and strong too." He flashed her a grin. "Now let's find a place to stop for the night."

She walked around to the front of the wagon on unsteady feet. Gideon put her in all sorts of knots by smiling at her, hell, just by breathing. He was definitely dangerous for her equilibrium and her heart, not to mention her peace of mind. Yet he was by her side, searching for her family. He was a Southern gentleman, something she thought had drowned in the blood from the Civil War.

Chloe was pensive and off-kilter as they made their way down the trail. The twilight gave way to darkness, and still they traveled in silence. It was okay with her, since she didn't know what to say to him anyway. How could she tell him that she wanted to travel by his side always? That they appeared to be meant to be together? It sounded foolish to her, and no doubt it would send him to the nearest saloon. Who would want a rough-talking, short, freckled, not-so-pretty orphan for a wife? She could bring nothing to a marriage except all her stellar qualities, or lack of them.

Her gloomy mood grew worse the farther they traveled. When he stopped the wagon, she peered into the night looking for whatever he'd spotted.

"What's going on?" Chloe was surprised to see how dark it had become while she'd been mooning over him in her mind.

"We're stopping. This is as good a place as any. I'm not risking the wagon or these old nags to get a few miles farther tonight. Let's set up camp in that field there. I hear water too, and we can wash up. Maybe even find another canteen in this mess in the morning."

Sounded like a fair plan, and Chloe was yet again glad he was there. She needed to regain her wits, and to do that she needed to steer clear of Gideon Blackwood.

Easier said than done.

They didn't speak as they set up their camp. Gideon built a fire close to the wagon, using it as a buffer for the wind and anything else that might try to visit them during the night.

As she unpacked the supplies to make supper, he used the quilt and blanket they'd made into packs to create a bedroll. There was no way they were going to sleep in the wagon with all the junk in there, not to mention the smell. He laid out only one bed—no matter what happened, it was the safest for both of them. He expected her to squawk about it, but she just glanced at him occasionally as she worked.

What was he to think of that? Was she hoping they would sleep together or apart? Perhaps she might even sleep in the wagon. He dismissed that idea. She was as repulsed as he was by the stench of the peddler woman's things. Gideon was out of his element and didn't know what to do or what to say.

Chloe chipped away at his control, and that made him short-tempered. He'd yelled at her enough to make her hate him, or at the very least dislike him. Yet she continued on with him, counting on him to help her find her family. He had already vowed in his heart to help her no matter what.

As he finished readying the bedroll, she gathered up a few things in the wagon, then appeared holding what looked to be a bedsheet. Her gaze settled on him, and the blankness in her eyes made him nervous.

"I'm going to wash up." She turned to go.

"No, you're not going anywhere alone." He rose and put his hands on his hips. "We're in a strange place, with obvious dangers no matter which way we turn. There's no way in hell I'm going to let you go off in the dark by yourself."

"I don't want you peeking at me. I don't need a protector." She kept walking away.

"Chloe. I said no."

She waved her hand in the air in dismissal.

Gideon thought perhaps his head would explode. "Chloe. Come back here."

All he saw was her back disappearing into the woods. He stomped after her, furious and scared at the same time. She tied him into knots. Gideon wasn't used to being disobeyed, and this little sprite was making him loco because she never listened to him.

"Don't be peeking at me." She had stopped by the creek, and from what he could see, she was glaring at him.

"I won't peek, and I resent the fact you believe I would." He didn't mean to sound affronted, but it came out that way.

"I don't know you from a hole in the ground, Mr. Blackwood. All we know is how to pleasure each other." Her brazen words left him speechless.

She disappeared behind some bushes, and he took the opportunity to check the water. The creek was about eight feet wide with a gentle current. He cupped a mouthful and tasted it, and it was clean. Next thing he knew, a pair of legs went past him into the water. She either didn't care if he peeked, or she hadn't seen him squatting by the edge.

Either way, he was struck dumb by the sight of Chloe Ruskin in the moonlight. Her skin was like alabaster, glowing against the darkness around her. She was perfectly formed, curved in all the right places, with a round behind, long legs and beautiful breasts. Gideon's dick tented in his trousers as he froze in place.

She scooped up sand from the bottom and started washing. He should back away and give her privacy. Yet something kept him there. She was like a selkie come to life, frolicking in the water and tempting him to join her. He shook his head to dispel the image and forced himself to creep backward. Unfortunately he stepped right on a stick that snapped with a loud crack.

"Are you peeking at me?"

He swallowed the lump in his throat and tried to come up with a reasonable response. "I was making sure you were safe."

She hmphed and kept washing. "Then throw me my clothes

over yonder so I can get them clean."

Gideon rose, painfully aware of the throbbing erection between his legs, and found her clothes on a bush. The rough fabric should be burned, but he didn't want to leave her with nothing to wear, however appealing that might be. He threw the clothes to her, and she murmured a thank-you.

With a tremendous amount of self-control, he turned his back to the sight of the incredibly delicious Chloe Ruskin naked in the water. He made himself recite Latin verbs in his head, leftovers from a childhood of schooling he never used. Then he recited recipes from the restaurant silently until he clenched his teeth so tight, he gave himself a headache.

"I'm done." She breezed past him and the bush she'd laid her wet clothes on. To his shock, she wore only a bedsheet.

Gideon forgot how to think at all.

Her hair hung down her back like a dark curtain, framing her small shoulders. Dry, it sprang up into curls, but wet it was longer than he'd expected. She was slender, as though she would break if he dared to touch her again. It was an illusion though, because he knew how strong she was, probably the strongest woman he'd ever met. That hardness was tempered with what he could only think of as innocence. She seemed young and had experienced quite a bit due to the war, but whatever was happening between them, he sensed she was out of her element.

Her scent finally hit him, and his body clenched all at once. Chloe was rough around the edges, but she was a blossom in the briar patch. He just had to get through the prickers and reach her.

Gideon picked up her clothes from the bush and followed her. There was no other choice since she wouldn't be safe alone and half-naked, yet he knew he was lying to himself if that was the only reason. She was a siren, a selkie calling him to her, and dammit to hell, he was helpless to resist.

It appeared the captain had met his colonel.

She sat in the firelight, finger-combing her wet hair. The bedsheet didn't do much to disguise her shape. He couldn't quite see through it, but his imagination and memory painted the picture of her naked form anyway. His dick grew another inch, and he had to squat by the fire or risk her noticing just how much he appreciated her near nakedness.

"Feel better?" His voice was rusty-sounding. Fool.

"Cleaner anyway." She disappeared behind the wagon, and all he could see was her feet.

He told himself not to follow her, to give her respect instead of lusting after her like an idiot with no brain. With a painful thud, he sat on the hard ground and poked at the fire that had burned down a bit while they'd been at the water. The coals glowed orange in the darkness, and he didn't take his eyes off them. Where he looked was something he could control. At least until she decided to parade around completely naked.

Gideon focused on his breathing until he was calmer. When she stepped back into view, he used every ounce of self-control he had not to look at her. The hard truth was he was fascinated by her, drawn to her, and it made him angry—at himself mostly. He'd spent too much time trying to find out exactly what his purpose was in life, leaving Tanger to find out where he belonged. Now he was losing his grip on all of it, including his self-control. Chloe muddied the waters too much. He needed to stop thinking about her, obsessing about her and certainly bedding her.

Chloe wasn't sure what to think of Gideon's behavior. He almost seemed nervous, which had to be impossible for the hard-nosed man. She told him not to follow her, yet he did, and then he acted odd. She needed to get clean, and if it offended him, so be it. Perhaps he hadn't had to wash up out-of-doors much since he was from a rich family.

She had found a few surprisingly clean men's shirts and trousers in the wagon. Now after a little while of airing on the side of the wagon, they'd be perfect to wear. Whoever they had belonged to had been short like Chloe; perhaps they might also fit. They weren't made for her, but free clothes were never turned away, especially after the war. She pulled on the trousers first and realized she'd need a rope to hold them up.

Now she was in a tight spot. The rope was somewhere in the wagon, Gideon had thrown it in there, and it was too dark to find it. They'd used the only other rope to secure the animals. If she put on the shirt, the trousers would fall to her feet. However, she couldn't parade around with nothing on but a pair of too-big trousers, or she would be shaking her titties at him. She decided to simply put the shirt on, and the trousers be damned. It was long enough to extend to her knees and covered most of her.

As Chloe came back around to the firelight, she thought a butterfly had landed in her stomach and flapped its wings. He stared at the flames, which was good. She didn't want him ogling her bare legs anyway.

"You hungry?"

A grunt was his only response. She went over to the edge of the wagon and picked up the pack with the coffee pot and pans in it. The next ten minutes helped her relax. She brewed coffee and whipped up a batch of cornpone. The meal made things appear almost normal. Still, he did not look at her. She felt silly and suspicious at the same time.

"Coffee's ready." She poured herself a cup and sat back to

sip it. The other tin cup waited on the rock beside the fire. "You sick or something?"

He finally turned to look at her, and she felt like she'd been burned by the coals. There was so much heat coming from his blue eyes, her breath caught in her throat. He took his time staring at her legs, her body, then her face, and she thought for sure she'd melt like butter on a skillet.

Holy God.

Chloe resisted the urge to fan herself, although the air between them must've been a hundred degrees. "I, uh, made coffee."

"I realize that."

"Don't you want any?" She tugged at the shirt, wishing it was a bit longer.

"I'm too hot to drink coffee." His voice was husky, nearly a low growl.

She was like a rabbit facing a wolf. With every bit of strength she had, Chloe looked away. "H-how about cornpone?"

"I'm not hungry for food."

Oh boy. She managed to swallow some dry spit and pull out two tin plates from the pack. When she was looking for the knife to cut with, he appeared beside her. She let out a yelp and started so bad, she dropped the plates on her foot.

"Don't be scared, Chloe."

"I ain't scared." At least, she wasn't scared of him anyway. No, she was afraid of her body's reaction to his nearness and the way she swayed toward him without hesitation. Chloe had never felt such things before.

He reached up and cupped her cheek, his calloused thumb caressing her skin. "You are the most maddening, sassy, amazing woman I've ever met. You are driving me loco, you know that? I made a promise to myself to stop touching you, and then you appear in that shirt."

Chloe didn't know what to say. He thought she was amazing?

"I am going to be a gentleman if it kills me, but I wanted to ask your permission for a kiss." He leaned closer, his breath whispering across her lips.

She couldn't have denied him if she wanted to. "Kiss me already, you foolish man."

It wasn't what she expected. He brushed his lips across hers, the barest touch, then pulled away. She wanted to grab him and pull him close, press her lips to his and release the pent-up passion beating like a drum in her chest. Yet she didn't and Chloe cursed her own cowardice. Looking him in the eye, she lost the courage she had used in the darkness of the night to climb into the wagon.

"The cornpone is burning."

His observation was like a bucket of ice water on a hot day. She gasped and reached for the pan, only to have him grab her arm.

"No need to burn yourself. Use the rag."

Shaking, she accepted that he'd saved her from a nasty injury. Her own stupidity left her careless. With a grateful, weak smile, she used the rag to pull the pan from the side of the fire. It wasn't too burned, just crispy on the bottom. With efficiency born of familiarity, she sliced it up and placed it on the tin plates, giving him two-thirds of it.

"I said I wasn't hungry."

She rolled her eyes. "And I don't rightly care. You need food to keep going, and I ain't letting you get the vapors 'cause you haven't eaten."

His mouth twitched as if he was holding back a laugh, but he didn't protest again. He took the plate, then, using the same rag, he grabbed the pot and poured himself coffee. This time when he sat across from her, the tension between them had eased enough to where the little hairs on her arms didn't stand up anymore.

"I made one bedroll."

She glanced at it. "I saw." In fact, she was wondering why but wanted to see what he would say without asking him.

"Is that okay with you?"

She shrugged. "It makes no never mind. It's a bed, which is better than shivering under a tree with just leaves to keep you warm." As soon as she said it, she glanced at him to see his reaction. Chloe hadn't meant to let that slip. He looked startled.

"It surely does." He took a bite of cornpone, chewed and swallowed before he spoke again. The man had stellar table manners. "You've slept under a tree before, then?"

Well, she had to admit it. After all, it was she who brought it up.

"Yep."

He nodded, and she was pleased he didn't ask her for details. That's when it hit her. He didn't ask because he knew how it felt—an unspoken bond she hadn't expected. This soldier from the south had likely endured things he would never admit to. It surprised and intrigued her, but she didn't pursue questioning him about it. He'd done her the same courtesy.

They ate the rest of their meager dinner in silence. The sounds of the night surrounded them, soothing her frayed nerves, and surprisingly, when she finished eating, she was sleepy. She had thought it would be hours before she felt tired enough to sleep. The day had been long and fraught with worry and stress, and it all weighed down on her. Before she could stop it, a jaw-cracking yawn hit her.

The corner of his mouth quirked up. "Tired?"

"No." Then, damn it, she yawned again.

"Me neither." He surprised her by picking up the supper dishes. "I'll be back in ten minutes."

Chloe stared after him, watching his lean-hipped swagger until the darkness swallowed him completely. Gideon was dangerous to her heart, and she knew it. If she were honest with herself, he had set himself a nice spot deep in her heart already.

She sighed as she rose to her feet. Granny wasn't here to talk to and help figure out the tangled mess inside her. Something told her Gideon was the perfect man for her, but she didn't want to fall in love yet. She had to take care of her family. They always came first, no matter what. Her own feelings for Gideon Blackwood would have to be second.

With a heavy heart, she crawled into the bedroll and was asleep in a blink.

Chapter Six

Chloe was just a lump beneath the blanket when he returned. He wondered if she were playing possum, but then heard a soft snore and realized she was asleep. Gideon shook with exhaustion. Every bone and muscle in his body was sore as if he'd been beaten during the day. It was definitely an emotional beating, if not a physical one. A day of ups and downs, absolute lunacy in the purest sense of the word.

He set the dishes down, added a couple more logs to the fire to keep it going for a while, then turned to the bedroll. Perhaps he expected her to look young and innocent in her sleep. But she didn't. Chloe's hair was splayed out like a fan, sparkling red and gold in the firelight. Her lips were slightly parted as though waiting to be kissed. The shirt gaped open as she lay on her side, revealing the barest hint of the curve of her breast.

Blood surged into his dick, and he hardened in seconds. He forced himself to take deep breaths and not to touch her until he was more in control of himself. She was a slip of a thing, beauty in an unconventional wrapper. After all the women his friends had fallen in love with, Gideon had expected to find a simple woman to live a quiet, happy life with.

He held back the snort with great effort. His experiences with Chloe had been nothing short of a disaster, yet he was drawn to her. There was a bond there, one that grew stronger with each passing hour. He hadn't intended on falling in lust or love with a traveling smart-mouthed, short woman from Virginia, but damned if both hadn't happened.

Gideon sat down to take off his boots, then crawled in next to her, careful to stay above the blanket. His body still throbbed with the need to touch her, and the clean scent emanating from her side of the bedroll made it worse. He rolled over and gave her his back, but it didn't help. His dick knew exactly where she was.

"Tell me about where you came from." Her words startled him.

"Jesus, woman, I thought you were sleeping."

"I was, but I sleep light. Had to learn to." She was right, of course; women traveling alone could not afford to sleep heavy or risk their safety and perhaps their lives for it. "Tell me about where you came from."

He felt peevish enough to be difficult. "You first."

A small fist landed on his shoulder. "You're a hard man, Gideon Blackwood."

This time his chuckle was a strangled grunt. "You have no idea."

After a moment, she started speaking. "I grew up in the middle of Virginia, not too far from West Virginia. My parents had a tobacco farm, and we scraped by on what we had. Granny is my daddy's ma. She lived with us after Mama died. I must've been about two, so I don't remember much before she was there." Her voice was soft and melodic, amazingly calming Gideon's over-stimulated body. "I have, I mean had a brother. He was two years older than me, and we were best friends growing up. We climbed trees, caught frogs, went swimming in the pond out back. Heck, I was eight before I realized I wasn't a boy like him."

"That explains a lot."

The fist thumped his shoulder again. "Hush up or I won't keep talking."

He swallowed back the words that threatened to pop out of his mouth. After all, if she wasn't talking, he'd be kissing her. He'd already vowed not to bed her again, but it was a damn hard vow to keep.

"Adam was a good brother, I think. He would tease me like big brothers do, but he let me tag along with our cousin Tobias when they went fishing. Then they enlisted together, and I ain't seen them since they left. My daddy died a year later, leaving me and Granny behind. We held on to the farm, but the world around us fell to pieces." She sighed long and hard. "We decided to head to Texas to live with Granny's sister. Right before we headed out, I found the girls hiding in a broken-down barn on their farm. Their mama had died at least a week before. Poor things."

She didn't describe what she'd found, and he didn't want to hear it. There was no need to explain since he could picture what the little moppets had endured. The war had destroyed the childhood of every American youth.

"What happened to your brother?"

"I don't know what happened to him, and like I told you before, he wasn't on the death notices. I looked every damn day for two years. I like to think he died a hero in battle, that way I don't have to think about him and Tobias dying alone in a ditch."

Gideon turned over. Her face was a pale oval in the meager light. "If you loved them, they couldn't have died alone. You were in their hearts."

Her eyes widened, and he was shocked to see they were

suspiciously wet. "Thank you for that."

His own throat grew tight at the raw emotion in her voice. He knew that kind of pain well, lived with it for five years, denied it every day too. Chloe was all kinds of trouble for him.

"Now it's your turn."

He grimaced and took her hand, which was soft and small in his. She rubbed the back of his hand with her thumb. It helped him start talking.

"I was born in Georgia, the only child of a cotton plantation owner and a Southern belle from one of the oldest society families in the state. My father was always disappointed in the fact I didn't want to run the plantation or follow in his footsteps. He tried charming me to take over for him, and when that didn't work, he tried force." Gideon had to pause and swallow back the old bitterness before it spilled out over Chloe. "I had everything money could buy, including tutors, clothes, horses and cigars. The one thing I didn't buy was friends. My cousins Zeke and Lee were there, along with Jake. I know he's actually my half brother, but Pa never admitted it. He was a tough son of a bitch who fathered bastards on the help and denied them. But I knew from the moment I met him that Jake was his—we have the same eyes. Then there's Nate. He's not related by blood, but he grew up with us, son of the town drunk. The one thing we had in common was being failures in the eyes of our fathers. No matter how much we tried, we could never please them."

"It don't matter what your daddy thinks. It's what you think that's important." Chloe was a tiny philosopher.

"I can say that out loud as many times as I want, but that doesn't mean I can accept it." He blew out a breath and chased away the ghosts riding his back. "My friends were my family, both by blood and by bonds stronger than it. We enlisted together too, and somehow we were all alive when the war was over." Gideon thought back to the day they left to fight and how confident they all were. Naïve, stupid boys.

"Alive, but not?"

He closed his eyes and forced back the dam of emotion she threatened to smash to bits *again*. It took him a minute to be able to speak, and his voice had grown huskier.

"We left Georgia for Texas. We had nothing left at home but death and destruction. Tales of a new life, a new start, tempted us. It took a hard year of traveling, working, breaking our backs for nothing, starving until we thought we'd made the biggest mistake of our lives. Then we found Tanger, a town in worse shape than us, if you can believe it." He chuckled at the thought, true as it was. "It was like the town was waiting for us to get there, and we just kind of fit together like puzzle pieces. We've been there two years now, and I don't think I'd want to live anywhere else. It's home."

"Then why did you leave? You had someplace else better to get to?"

Her question hit him like a rock to the chest. Why was he leaving the place he'd finally found? Tanger was *home*. Visiting Nate was always a good trip to make, but he had run from Tanger, and his friend's ranch was the nearest to escape to.

The truth tumbled out of his mouth before he could stop it. "I was running from myself."

Chloe didn't press him for more. "As much as I hate to say this, I'm glad you did, or I'd be alone. I reckon you might throw that back in my face, but it's said now."

Gideon hadn't considered what would have happened to the Ruskins if he hadn't been there. If he had still been in Tanger, Chloe would be alone, with no one to help her get her family back. Heck, she could even be dead, since whoever took

Granny and the girls might have gotten rid of the smart-mouthed hostage. He didn't want to think about the possibilities. He had to accept that something had sent him to find her.

The thought made his heart hiccup.

His brain told him there was no such thing as fate or being sent by an unseen force. As an ex-soldier, he believed in what he could see and touch, yet he did rely on his instincts. They'd saved his life more than once. That conflicted with his common sense. The thoughts whirled around in his head until he had to press his hand to his temple to stop them.

What he did know was that he accepted his responsibility for Chloe and her family. Exactly what that meant, he didn't want to know. He had to stop questioning why, or he might really go loco.

He saw her shiver in the near darkness. Without asking permission, he pulled her close, tucking her against him like they were a pair of spoons. She fit perfectly, he was startled to note, and their combined body heat stopped her shivering. Gideon settled the blanket over both of them, and to his surprise, sleep claimed him.

She woke suddenly, but she wasn't scared or startled. For the first time she could remember, Chloe was warm and safe, protected. She'd slept beside Granny most of her life since there wasn't a whole lot of room at the farmhouse. During the trip to Texas, she became used to sleeping with the two little girls pressed on either side of her. Yet none of those experiences made her feel like she did waking up wrapped in Gideon's arms.

Since she'd met Gideon, nothing had been familiar, emotionally or physically. She'd felt things she'd never imagined, experienced things that set her flying to the stars and crashing to the earth. Up until this point in her life, there hadn't been much she could rely on, but she knew in her heart she could count on him. This stranger, this man who happened to be in the same place at the same time, had changed her life in a few short days.

It was a sobering thought and one that made her pull away from the cocoon of his arms. She had no right to be there, no future with him, no matter how much she might wish it. After they found Granny and the girls, Gideon and Chloe would be strangers again. This experience would seem like a dream, one she could replay in her mind for the rest of her life.

His scent filled her with each breath she took in. It was a pleasant, manly smell she could definitely get used to. Her behind was snuggled up against his man parts, and although they weren't hard, Chloe's body stirred from the sensation of just touching him. She didn't expect that, yet given her wanton behavior on the wagon, she should have. The man drove her to be a hussy, and damned if she didn't like it. However, finding her family was more important than scratching her itch to make love with him again.

Make love. It wasn't quite an apt description of what they'd done, but it felt right to her. Chloe had never been attracted enough to a man before to want to do more than kiss him. And now she wanted to yank his trousers down and do all kinds of amazing things over and over. She knew it wasn't right, and even as her body heated at the thought, her mind pulled her back. Chloe swore her nipples complained at the craving for his touch and his tongue, not that he was hers to lose.

Pitiful as could be, she extricated herself from his arms and shivered in the cool morning air. She'd forgotten she was wearing only a man's shirt. As she was padding barefoot toward the creek, she stopped in her tracks. Last night she'd left her dress and underthings on a bush by the water to dry. They were now draped over another bush close enough to the fire to have dried completely. The man would never stop surprising her.

She took her clothes and went down to the creek to wash and piss. A mist hung over the top of the gentle water, giving it an eerie look. A shiver shot straight up her spine, and she hugged herself to stop it. What was she afraid of? There wasn't anybody around, and Gideon was sleeping twenty feet away. The feeling persisted though, and she rushed through cleaning up and yanked on her clothes. They were a little stiff from being cold, but at least they were clean and dry.

A small regret niggled at her. She shouldn't have left him lying there asleep and alone. If Granny were there, she would have told Chloe to follow her heart and be with him again. But Granny wasn't there and that was the reason Chloe hadn't followed through with the urge to be with him. She had to find her family, rescue them from whatever monsters had taken them. It was war, and she had to be a good soldier.

A twig snap brought every nerve ending to life. It didn't come from the direction of the wagon, so it wasn't Gideon. She crouched down, reaching for the knife in her boot, only to realize she was still barefoot. Her boots were with Gideon. She was unarmed but surely not helpless. Chloe searched the ground for a sturdy branch. No chance she would give up without a fight. She wrapped her hand around the thickest stick she could find and waited. Her heart pounded as the twig snap turned into footsteps, stealthy ones to be sure, but she could hear them. Gideon had taught her that—to stop and listen in utter silence. She'd thank him later, if she was still alive.

The steps grew closer and closer, pausing, then restarting. She was going to stand up and start screaming like a wild woman if whoever it was didn't get on with it. Finally they stopped just five feet from her hiding place. She gripped the stick, her breath coming in short, soundless gasps, then stood.

She raised the stick and swung with all her might, only to recognize the back of Gideon's head just seconds before she knocked him on his ass.

"Jesus Christ, Chloe," Gideon howled as he clutched his head. "What the hell are you doing?"

She threw the branch and dropped to her knees. "Oh shit, Gideon, I'm sorry." She reached for his head, but he batted her hand away. Chloe told herself not to be hurt by the gesture. After all, she'd just conked him. Hard.

He glared at her. "When you didn't come back to the camp, I thought something had happened to you. Hell, woman, did you have to hit me so hard?"

"I thought you were one of the kidnappers or worse." She ached to touch him, soothe the hurt she'd inflicted, but she just sat there and accepted his well-deserved scolding. "I'm sorry."

"I guess I don't have to worry about you getting hurt, then. If all you had was a stick and you managed to crack my skull, you don't even need your knife."

She spotted her knife on the ground by his feet. He had gotten concerned and gone looking for her. It wasn't a big gesture, but damned if it didn't make her lose control.

For the first time since her family had gone missing, Chloe burst into tears.

Gideon watched her from the corner of his eye. After her surprising tears and the knock on his head—which still hurt— he didn't know what she was thinking. Just when he thought he had her figured out, she did something unexpected. Like crying. Of all the women he'd known in his life, Chloe was the last person he expected to break down like that. She was tougher than he was, for God's sake.

She had pointed at the knife, then at his head and cried some more. He hadn't known what to do but hand her his handkerchief and wait. She had gotten to her feet with the knife and handkerchief in hand and left him sitting on the forest floor with his head throbbing and his mind whirling. She had caught him off guard with the stick, but there was no real damage to speak of, although he'd probably be picking bark out of his hair for a few days.

By the time he made it back to camp, she had stopped crying. She had also packed the bedrolls, made coffee and put the leftover cornpone out to eat. He ate gratefully, keeping an eye on her, wondering what she was thinking. If she was more like every other woman, he might have asked her why she had cried, but he didn't dare. They needed each other, and he was already on uncharted ground with her.

They packed up and were on their way before the sun was fully up. He was glad of the daylight and picked up a set of wagon tracks straight off.

"Do you see anything?" Her voice was a bit rusty, and he thought it might have been due to the hysterics earlier but didn't think it wise to say anything.

"There's some tracks but not fresh ones. At least twelve hours old." He pointed at the side of the trail where the grass had grown high. "Keep your eye on the grass. If you see any that's been trampled or stepped on, let me know."

She nodded and focused intently on her task, giving him a chance to study her. Chloe's face was drawn, with circles under her eyes and a tightness to her mouth that made her lips almost white. The clouds obscured the sun, and she hadn't put her hideous hat on. The light breeze tickled the explosion of curls on her head.

She was beautiful. *Beautiful.*

Gideon stared at her, rendered mute by his recognition of just how lovely Chloe Ruskin was. Her beauty struck him between the eyes, stealing his thoughts. He could imagine waking up to her every morning, being able to stroke her freckled skin and kiss her plump lips. It would be a life he could love. Hell, a woman he could love.

His throat went dry, and the world beneath him shifted. Gideon knew what he was thinking, feeling and accepting. Well, holy hell. He did need to leave home to find where, and with whom, he belonged.

With Chloe Ruskin.

He should be smart enough not to let her go now that he'd found her. But he hadn't ever fallen in love before, and his experience with women was limited enough to make him into an idiot.

She scowled so hard her eyebrows touched, and he had the urge to wipe away her unhappiness. "There, do you see it?"

He shook himself as if waking from a dream. "What?"

"There. Right there." She smacked his arm. "Stop the damn wagon."

With a quick yank on the reins, the horses came to a shuddering stop, not that they were going very fast anyway.

"What do you see?"

"A ribbon." She jumped down before she even finished speaking.

He wanted to chastise her for nearly breaking her legs and running pell-mell away from the wagon, but he didn't. She wasn't one of his soldiers and she sure as hell wasn't going to listen to him. He had no time to ponder what it might mean if she became his wife, because she stood up and whooped like a raider.

It surprised the hell out of him.

"Martha! I know it was Martha. She's the one who always thinks up trouble, but she's real smart." Chloe held up a scrap of blue clutched in her fingers. "She tied a piece of ribbon to this bush."

He glanced at the tattered-looking ribbon. "Are you sure? It looks like it's been hanging there quite some time."

She shook her fist. "I am absolutely sure. We bought the girls this ribbon right before we left Virginia. It's the same shade of blue as their eyes. We could only buy one length, and the girls split it between them." She pulled his face down and kissed him hard. "We found their trail!"

He hardly had time to react before she went barreling through the brush looking for more signs. In no time, they'd found the campsite with the ashes not quite cool. The grass on the side of the road was beaten down as if there had been something heavy resting on it.

Gideon smiled grimly at Chloe. "We found their trail."

She whooped again, waving that tiny scrap of blue as if she had found a fortune in gold. He scooped her up and flipped her on his shoulder, carrying her back to the wagon as she protested loudly.

"What in tarnation are you doing?" She punched his back hard enough to make him wince.

He set her on the seat to stop any more protests. Then he kissed her, catching her breath of surprise in a hot meeting of their lips.

"Getting back on the trail so we can find your family."

She rewarded him with a wide smile on her flushed face.

"Then let's hit that trail, Blackwood."

Gideon jumped into the wagon and used as much gusto as he could to get the nags moving. They were back on the scent.

He thought perhaps they would find more evidence of the kidnappers, but as the day wore on, they encountered nothing but dirt and a faint set of tracks. It was something but not much. Chloe's jubilation at finding Martha's ribbon waned as the afternoon faded into evening. It was hot and uncomfortable, and they needed real food. The meager supplies they had were nearly gone, and if they didn't find sustenance soon, they might not ever catch up with the Ruskin family.

His stomach yowled loud enough it scared some birds out of a tree. Chloe looked at him askance but didn't say anything. They had nothing but a few strips of jerky, some coffee beans and whatever water they could find. It wouldn't last another day.

"We can catch a rabbit or something." She touched the butt of the rifle. "I'm a good shot."

"I don't want to stop just yet. We still have a bit more daylight left."

She nodded, and he had a feeling she was grateful. Every minute they spent looking was another minute her family didn't have to spend with whatever bastards took them. He could have wept when he saw the buildings in the distance.

Miraculously they'd arrived at a town.

"Where are we?"

"I don't know, never been this way, but I'm guessing they'll have supplies." He glanced at her weary face. "We need supplies."

She shook her head. "I don't have any money. Hell, Gid, everything I owned was on that wagon or back in the field where we left the furniture." She looked away. "I don't have anything."

He took her hand, turned it palm up and placed a kiss in the center. "You have me."

Her mouth fell open, and her eyes reflected confusion and what he dared to guess was hope.

"You just want your horse back."

He kissed her forehead next. "I think Domino would be fine without me."

"Domino? That's his name?" She snorted softly. "I had that all wrong."

By the time he kissed her mouth, his breath was ragged and his body practically begged to be with her. "No, you've got it all right."

To his surprise, she pushed him back. "Don't get all cow-eyed on me, Blackwood. We've got a long road to travel before we're done."

He stared into her narrowed eyes and realized he'd acted like an ass. Chloe seemed to have that effect on him. Where the hell was his famous captain's ability to focus? It was as if she'd thrown a bucket of water on him. He was shocked but stupidly grateful. His brother or cousins would have told him what an ass he'd been if they'd been there. Now it fell to a little slip of a woman with a harsh mouth and a stiff spine.

"You're right."

She raised one brow. "Don't think I've heard that before."

He nodded tightly. "I assure you that you won't hear it again."

Chloe waved a hand toward the town. "Get a move on, then. Time is ticking away."

Gideon slipped away from his own confusion, shutting the door on it until they accomplished what they'd set out to do. He rode into town with the eye of a trained soldier, taking in the sleepy feel of it, the well-swept wood-planked sidewalks and the curtains in the windows. It had the air of a safe place, but he would remain on guard.

They stopped the wagon at the end of the street next to the mercantile. The livery was close by as well. Chloe looked around with more suspicion than he did. He still wished the Devils were there with him too and not just one small, ornery woman.

"What now?"

He jumped down, and before he could get to the other side of the wagon, she was down and waiting for him. With a frown, he took her arm.

"We'll go into the mercantile and make friends, so be a good girl and pretend we're happily married."

As they walked in, a small bell tinkled over the door. She pinched him under the arm hard enough to make his eyes water. Instead of annoying him, her gesture made him smile. She was a warrior, full of fight and life.

His boots thunked on the well-swept but worn floor. It wasn't the largest store he'd been in, but it was neat and looked cared for. A young man appeared from behind a blue-curtained doorway on the left.

"Evening, folks." He stepped toward them.

Gideon took the man's measure and saw nothing in his stance or demeanor that suggested he was a threat. "Good evening. I'm Gideon Blackwood and this is my wife, Chloe."

She accidentally stepped on his foot. "Pleased to meetcha."

"Likewise, Mrs. Blackwood. I'm Joseph Newton. What can I help you with?" The stranger's blue gaze was guileless.

"We were ambushed about two days back. We lost our money and my good horse. I was hoping there was a bank in town, and I could get some money wired to me to buy new supplies."

The man nodded, his black curls bobbing with the movement. "Sure thing. Ambrose Moore runs the bank. He's likely still there. Why don't I take you over there, and Mrs. Blackwood can start getting what you all need."

Gideon glanced down at her. She looked like she had no idea how to even pick a spool of thread much less what was needed for a hard trail ride.

"You have someone who can help her?"

"Yup, my wife Daisy is upstairs taking care of her daddy. This used to be his store." Joseph stepped toward the curtain and pulled it back. "Daisy, can you come down and help some folks?"

Gideon heard a faint feminine response, then the sound of footsteps coming down the stairs. When Mrs. Newton appeared, he couldn't help but smile. She was as small as Chloe, with light brown hair, a bit plumper, but she could help his "wife" pick out clothes that would fit her.

"Mrs. Newton, my name's Gideon Blackwood and this is my wife, Chloe. I'd be grateful if you could help her pick out new clothes, any sundries she needs and food for a week's trail ride on horseback." He tipped his hat, and she smiled broadly, her apple cheeks rosy in the evening light.

"Sure thing, Mr. Blackwood. I'd be happy to help." She stepped toward the corner of the store stocked full of ready-made clothes, but Chloe didn't follow.

"I don't need no clothes." Her fierce whisper was meant for his ears only.

"Yes, you do. You need a split skirt to ride, and I would actually pay her to burn that thing you're wearing." He leaned down, seemingly to kiss her cheek, but instead he bit her earlobe.

She jumped a few inches and stared at him with wide eyes.

"Spend as much as you want. We're not leaving here until you have the clothes you need."

"You're loco, Gid."

"I've heard that before."

He turned to follow Joseph out of the store before she could say another word. Gideon glanced back and was pleased to see Chloe over by the clothing while Mrs. Newton chattered away at her.

Chloe had never bought ready-made clothes before. Heck, she'd never even touched them before. The storekeeper's wife was friendly enough, but she was pulling out all kinds of frilly things Chloe wasn't sure what to do with.

She finally had to say something, much as it pained her. "My husband and me ain't been married long. I don't know much about how to dress proper."

Daisy stopped and regarded her with her pretty brown eyes. "Don't worry, Mrs. Blackwood. I can show you everything you need to know."

Chloe wasn't sure what "everything" meant, but she nodded anyway. Then her lesson began in how ladies dressed. There were layers and layers, plus something called a corset—which she refused to wear—and lacy stuff until she thought she'd run from the store.

When Daisy pulled out a simple cotton chemise and drawers, Chloe was grateful to see just how plain they were.

"Those two."

The shopkeeper frowned at them. "Are you sure? These are just cotton."

"I'm sure. I don't need anything fancy." She took the garments from Daisy, surprised by how soft they were.

"Now you're about the same height as me, so I know what will fit you." Daisy fussed around for a few minutes, pulling out a few dresses, skirts and blouses. She stopped and snapped her fingers. "I know just the thing. One of the rancher's wives makes leather clothing for me to sell. She made this riding skirt last year, but it's too small for most everyone. It was a leftover piece of leather, and she thought maybe someone would buy it for their daughter. Nobody did."

Daisy dug around on a shelf until she pulled out the most beautiful skirt Chloe had ever seen. It was the color of butternut squash, obviously well tanned and softened. She reached out to touch it and found it softer than the cotton undergarments in her hand.

"It's beautiful." Her voice was barely above a whisper.

"It's yours." Daisy handed it to her. "I never thought I'd sell it, and I know Beatrice would be glad someone would get use out of it."

"I can't take this without paying for it." Chloe rubbed her cheek on the leather, breathing in its rich scent.

"You'll pay for everything else, so we'll just call this one a gift for a weary traveler." Daisy smiled. "Now let's get you a blouse to wear, a couple dresses, stockings and some boots. Then we'll work on supplies for your trail ride."

Chloe hadn't met anyone like Daisy before, but she liked her. She was honest, nice and respectful, didn't treat her as if she was lower than dirt, like some folks did. Whether it was due to the promise of Gideon's money or the woman's innate goodness, Chloe wasn't sure she wanted to know.

After a brief conversation and a wire to Tanger, the banker

gave Gideon a letter of credit to use with the merchants in town as well as one hundred dollars cash. He'd had only ten dollars of travel money, and he'd needed a lot more to get what they needed. Besides, he'd already decided to give the Ruskins money for the rest of their journey. It was the first step in not feeling helpless anymore. After he sent a wire to Nate to let him know he wasn't coming, he sent another to Zeke. Having a sheriff as a cousin had its advantages.

"Anything else I can help you with?" Joseph Newton had stayed with him the entire time it took to get everything done. They were walking back toward the mercantile.

"I have a wagon we found abandoned in the woods. It looks like a peddler's wagon, but it's in rough shape, smells like an outhouse in the sun." Lying to the folks who were helping him didn't sit well, but he couldn't very well tell the man he'd stolen it. Gideon stopped and tipped his hat back. "I don't know what to do with it, but I thought maybe I could trade it to the livery for a couple horses."

"Let's go see if Frank is there. He owns the livery here in Westville and has a few horses he keeps for renting to folks." Once again, the shopkeeper proved to be invaluable.

Frank was an older German man with a thick accent, big arms and an even bigger chest. He was soft-spoken but eyed Gideon with great consideration after the offer of the wagon. Joseph was there to vouch for him as well.

"I saw it there and wondered. I've seen it before." The blond giant stared hard at Gideon. "It belong to a hag who smell bad. She cheated me when she sold me tools last year."

Gideon took a breath. "It still smells like her."

Frank laughed. "Then I chop it up and burn it. Her nags will be good for ladies and the *kinder* to ride. Nice and slow."

Gideon suspected Frank didn't believe his story about

finding the wagon, but Lady Luck had shined down on him. The hag had cheated one too many people.

"I appreciate the trade. There's a few quilts in the back with supplies that belong to us. I need to keep those, if you don't mind. I'll pay for saddles and full tack."

"Of course you will. I have good quality." Frank led him and Joseph to the corral to look at the horses.

Gideon found two bays that were perfect for them. One mare and one gelding, both young and healthy. The three of them chatted as Gideon inspected the tack. It was good quality, but he took his time examining each piece. He needed information.

"Two men took our wagon a couple days ago." He looked up at Frank and Joseph. "They took my wife's little sisters and grandmother too." He let that information sink in. "I think they were headed this way, near as we can tell. It's a big wagon with a canvas on it, raised up about four feet with a frame under it to let folks ride in the back. They probably left the girls and Granny with one of them, and the other would have ridden in for supplies." He watched both men carefully for any reaction. "Besides me and Chloe, have there been any strangers through here in the last day?"

Joseph shook his head. "They haven't stopped at the store."

Frank stroked his beard. "There was a man came in early this morning with a broken cinch strap. I repair it for him."

"What did he look like?" Gideon was in the dark about who he was dealing with. Hell, he didn't even know what their hair color was, how big they were or even their ages.

"Young man, a few years younger than you. He wore a hat, but what he had of a beard was light brown, pockmark scars on his face. Not as big as you, Mr. Blackwood, perhaps Joseph's size." Frank was clear about the details, and Gideon knew it was all true.

"Did he have an accent? Speak with a lisp or something like that?"

"Nothing like that. He sound like he's from anywhere."

"Did you see what direction he rode off in?" Gideon wanted to throw his fist in the air in triumph. This was the first sighting of one of the men he figured had taken the Ruskins.

"Southwest, out the end of town toward the river. It's about ten miles outside town." Frank narrowed his eyes. "You talk like a man of the law."

That made Gideon smile. "Former soldier is more like it. My cousin is the sheriff at home, and I'm afraid I fall into old habits."

"Good habits, I'm thinking." Frank gestured toward the south end of the street. "You should talk to sheriff here and get help."

"I will. Thank you for everything, Frank." He put his hands on two saddles. "I'll take both of these, with blankets. My wife is small, and we'll need to adjust the stirrups for her."

"She's about Daisy's size," Joseph added.

"I can get it all ready for you, Mr. Blackwood. Come back in thirty minutes."

Gideon thanked the man before he walked out with Joseph. "Where is the sheriff's office?"

"Will Cannon is the sheriff. He keeps the office at his house, the big white one at the end there." Joseph pointed down the street. "Do you want me to come with you?"

Gideon shook his head. "No need. I'll take care of this part myself. Please tell my wife I'll be there in a few minutes and that we leave in thirty."

After the shopkeeper went back toward the mercantile,

Gideon headed off to speak to the sheriff.

Chloe could have wept for the softness of the garments she now wore. Everything was comfortable and fit her as if someone had made them specially them for her. It was astonishing what the simple act of putting on new clothes did to her.

She felt like a woman.

Daisy smiled, her cheeks dimpling as she walked around Chloe. "You look lovely, Mrs. Blackwood." She turned to her husband, who was behind the counter tallying the items piled high in front of them. "Doesn't she, Joseph?"

"Almost as pretty as you." Joseph winked at his wife. "Your husband is going to be pleased as punch to see how you look, Mrs. Blackwood."

"Please call me Chloe. I don't think I'll ever answer to someone calling me missus."

"You said you haven't been married long?" Daisy's question made Chloe freeze in mid-motion. "I know it took me at least a year to get used to being called a missus myself."

"No, not long. Before we left Virginia, Gideon and I got hitched."

"Starting a new life in Texas?" Daisy's eyes were full of compassion as she took Chloe's hands.

It was odd to be holding hands with a stranger, but at the same time, it felt right. Chloe decided being with Gideon had scrambled her brain.

"Yes, something like that." She swallowed back the lump of emotion that appeared in her throat. Chloe could not afford to be weak, especially in front of this nice lady.

The door to the mercantile opened, and the tinkling of the bell sent a shiver down Chloe's spine.

"There you are, Mr. Blackwood. I was just telling your wife how lovely she looks." Daisy moved out of the way, leaving Chloe directly in Gideon's line of sight.

He stared at her, his blue eyes drinking her in, up and down, and again, until she thought she'd have to kick him. Gideon walked toward her, then circled her as he continued to stare.

"Much better than the burlap one."

She would kick him.

He picked her up, his arms holding her tight against his firm body. Leaning in until their noses touched, he spoke softly so only she could hear. "You're exquisite. The most beautiful thing I've ever seen."

His heart thumped against hers, and she knew he was telling her the truth. That silly lump decided to come back to her throat for a second time. This time it wasn't because of sadness.

"Let me down, you big oaf." She swatted at his shoulder, trying to regain control of the emotions running rampant through her.

He kissed her hard, twice, then set her on her feet. The grin he turned on the Newtons was nothing short of blinding.

"She looks perfect, Mrs. Newton. Now all she needs is a hat."

"I have a hat."

"She needs a hat that doesn't look like a cow turd." Gideon tipped his hat to Daisy. "Pardon my crude language."

Daisy giggled. "No need to apologize. I've seen the hat." She turned toward Chloe. "We already picked out a new one."

He picked up the chocolate brown hat that was sitting by the pile of supplies. After a brief examination he plopped it on her head.

He blew out a breath. "Now I'm in trouble."

This time when Chloe smiled, it was one of genuine happiness. Gideon's words, his gestures, his reactions, were gifts she never expected to receive in her lifetime. She *felt* beautiful and special, much more than she ever had before.

"The horses should be almost ready. Let's pack up the supplies and get going."

"You're not going to spend the night in town?" Joseph frowned. "It's almost dark."

Gideon glanced at her for approval, which made her feel ten feet tall. She nodded, pleased to see he considered her opinion before speaking.

"We need to keep going." Gideon shook the man's hand. "Thank you for everything, Joseph. I won't forget it."

Before Chloe knew what was happening, Daisy enfolded her in a hug. "Good luck, Chloe."

Gideon paid an astonishing amount of money for their supplies, more than she'd ever seen. She kept her surprise and her protests to herself though. Now wasn't the time to be taking him to task for overspending.

Within a few minutes, they headed toward the livery with their supplies packed neatly into small packages to fit into the saddlebags. A big blond giant with a beard greeted them, shaking hands with Gideon. Had he made friends with the entire town?

"It is a pleasure to meet you, Mrs. Blackwood."

Chloe managed to smile at him, although she had never been this friendly with strangers in her life. Thank goodness they were heading out of town.

"The horses are ready. I put your packs on the back of

each." Frank led them into the barn where the cool darkness took a few minutes to get used to. "Here is your horse. Her name is Lightning. The other is called Thunder. They had the same dam, but Thunder is two years older."

She was surprised to see a small mare saddled and waiting. Chloe had spent most of her time in the saddle on mules or packhorses, never on a beautiful horse like this. It was a day of new experiences and possibly new friends. She petted the horse's velvety neck and was rewarded with a snuffle to her belly.

"I think she likes you," Gideon teased as he loaded their supplies into the saddlebags. "Can't say as I blame her."

Chloe whispered in the horse's ear. "You ride like you're named, okay, girl? Help me find my family."

The horse's ears twitched as if she understood. Gideon put a mounting block beside the horse and motioned her to mount.

"Ready?"

"Let's go find those bastards." She ignored the livery owner's chuckle and focused on Gideon's tight smile.

"That's my girl." He made sure she got up into the saddle before he mounted his horse. Chloe was not surprised by his grace or agility. The man could do anything.

Maybe, just maybe, with him at her side, she could do anything too.

Chapter Seven

The rest of the evening passed quickly. They were both full of renewed energy, and riding a pair of good horses alleviated the feelings of helplessness. In fact, he felt better than he had in a long time, more alive. Much of it had to do with the woman at his side. Chloe had done her best to drag him into her world, voluntarily or not, and he was finally recognizing it was where he was supposed to be.

"It's almost dark."

"Even though I have more hair than a head should, I can actually see through it." Her sarcasm had grown sharper as the day wore on.

"If it's dark, they can't drive the wagon either."

"I know that." She sounded frustrated.

"We've made good time today, made up some ground. We'll start early and make up even more." Gideon hardened his voice. "We won't do them any good if we run into a gopher hole and cripple one of these fine horses."

She didn't look at him, but he saw her swallow. "I know. I just wish, it's silly, but I wish we could see them, know that we're getting closer. I wish…" She pointed ahead. "I see something, Gid."

It was the third time she'd used a shortened version of his

name. Hearing it from her lips was an unexpected gift, one that made his heart thump, one he wanted to hear again and again.

Chloe had an excellent seat on a horse, and she raced ahead on Lightning as if they were one being. She slid off the saddle with an ease he'd not seen from a woman before and dropped to her knees.

"Is it a ribbon?"

She held up another scrap of blue with a triumphant smile. "Yes! Martha, you clever little critter!"

Gideon smiled at Chloe. "That she is."

"We're getting closer, aren't we?" She got to her feet.

"Yes, we are. I need to tell you what I learned in town today. Let's make camp here. No doubt there is a good spot for a campfire, and I hear running water." He took both horses' reins.

She held the ribbon to her heart for a moment before she answered. "I don't want to, but I will because I know we need to."

Gideon could respect that, and he was powerful glad he didn't have to argue with her about when and where to stop. If he were honest with himself, he might have kept going through the night if he had been chasing his family's kidnappers. However, he had spent many nights on a horse and knew how to ride in the darkness with only the moon for a guide. Chloe had obviously spent a lot of time on a horse, but she likely hadn't ridden at night before. It could be more than dangerous for someone with no experience.

They set up camp as though they'd done it a hundred times instead of twice. Chloe built the fire while Gideon took care of the horses. He refilled the new large canteens they'd purchased in town in the small stream he found nearby. By the time he came back, she had coffee burbling on the fire and was using her knife to open a can of peaches.

"Don't take your thumb off with that thing. I don't feel like carrying you back to that town." He set the canteens down and then sat on the ground across from her.

"I can outshoot, outhunt, outskin and outcook any man alive." She speared him with a hard look. "You have no faith in me, Gideon Blackwood."

He stared at her, trying to see into her soul and find out what made her prickly. "I was joking with you, Chloe. You get your back up too easily."

"Joking?" Her mouth fell open. "What does that mean?"

"When people are friends, they joke with each other." He had no idea what her home life had been like growing up, just that it was hard and apparently left no room for fun.

"Are we friends?" Her voice had dropped, low and unsure.

His heart clenched at the life she must've led, since she didn't know how to laugh, how to be silly. He couldn't help but move over beside her. He took her hand and kissed the back of it, her skin warm against his lips.

"We will always be friends. No matter what."

She looked down at their joined hands. "I would like that."

Gideon told himself to stop kissing her hand, to go back to the other side of the fire, but damn if he ignored himself. Instead he settled next to her, a comfortable spot to be. They ate the peaches, some crackers and jerky, washing it all down with hot coffee.

When it came time to sleep, they crawled into a bedroll together. As they shared their body heat, the space beneath the blanket grew warmer, their breath white puffs in the cool night air. It was a form of torture he'd never thought to endure. Then again, there were a lot of things he hadn't considered until he met Chloe.

"Why don't you touch me no more?" Her soft question made him stop thinking of just how hard his dick was.

"What?"

She shifted her behind and it brushed against him, eliciting a small groan from deep in his throat.

"Like we did in the wagon and, um, on the wagon seat." She was silent for a moment. "Did I do a bad job? I don't have much experience, but it felt pretty good to me."

Gideon half-choked on the laugh that threatened. "Pretty good? Hell, Chloe, I spend my days trying not to think about how good it was."

The crickets sang around them as his cock thrummed in time with his heart.

"Oh. Well then, why don't we do it again?" She rolled over and looked at him in the meager light.

Gideon told himself they weren't married.

She wasn't a virgin before I met her.

Gideon told himself they were chasing dangerous people.

They have no idea they're being chased.

Gideon told himself there were a million other reasons to not touch her.

Can't even think of one.

He knew he shouldn't touch her, but it was damn hard, in more ways than one, not to.

"We shouldn't." His voice was tighter than a fiddle string.

"Why not?"

"Lots of reasons."

She chuckled, her breath caressing his face. "You sound like Granny when she can't think of a good reason to say no."

Chloe shifted closer until her breasts pillowed against his chest and her lips were inches from his. "I can think of one good reason to say yes."

Gideon shook with the force of his restraint. He inhaled, breathing her scent into his body, knowing he was fighting a losing battle. As soon as her lips touched his, there would be no more holding back.

"What reason is that?"

"Because I think I lo—"

His mouth came down on hers, cutting off her confession he was not ready to hear or accept. Her body, however, he was ready to accept and pleasure.

The dark, warm recesses of her mouth welcomed him, as her tongue danced and rasped against his. Her raised body heat and ragged breath told him she was as affected as he was. Gideon was embarrassed to notice he trembled when he touched her. After such a short time together, he was hopelessly tangled in her web with no escape in sight.

Her small hands crept down his arms, lightly squeezing as she went until he chuckled against her teeth.

"What are you doing?"

She bit at his lip. "Don't you dare make fun of me. I just like the way you feel. All hard and the like."

"More than you know, little one." He pressed his aching erection against her.

She sucked in a breath, which then hissed out from between her teeth. "Tell me that's not just a stick in your trousers, or I'm going to be real disappointed."

Gideon barked a laugh at her sassiness. "No, it's not just a stick." He kissed his way across her cheek, then nibbled on her earlobe. When he blew into her ear, she trembled against him.

"Good, because I'm feeling mighty ready to be close to you again, Gid." Her voice was rich with passion, something she had in abundance. Being intimate with him obviously brought it out in force.

Thank God.

He'd been with women before, but none as responsive or passionate as Chloe. She turned to melted butter in his arms, so soft and warm. Her nipples poked into his chest, hard and wanting. He had to have more.

Although he loved seeing her in her new clothes, he wanted to see her out of them now. He unbuttoned the shirt, kissing the exposed skin as he went. She smelled wonderful, like woman, sunshine and arousal. The perfect combination.

Her nipples were already pebbled, begging for his mouth. As soon as he pulled one into his mouth, her nails dug into his shoulders and she let loose a little moan. His dick must've grown another inch.

"That feels good, but I want more." Her hand crept around and she squeezed him. "Like this right here hiding in your drawers."

He bit her nipple even as her touch made him shudder. She sucked in another breath and squeezed him again. If she kept that up, he'd be done before he even got the damn drawers off. To save his dignity and please his lady, he shucked his clothes quickly, and then they were skin to skin.

He groaned as she spread her legs and his dick came in contact with the crisp hairs on her pussy. Gideon gritted his teeth to keep from coming all over her. When had he lost all self-control? Likely from the moment he'd touched Chloe Ruskin, or maybe even when he'd first laid eyes on her.

As he slid into her welcoming warmth, one thought ran through his head—she was made for him. They simply fit together. She closed around him. Her tightness mixed with the moisture from her arousal was a heady combination.

He kept his strokes slow at first, enjoying the gentle slide of their bodies. She pulled at his back, urging him to go faster, but he held back. Gideon wanted this to be something other than fumbling in the dark or a quick fuck on a wagon seat. He wanted to make love to her.

Heat radiated out from their joining, sapping all coherent thought. She scratched at him again, and he sped up his pace. They had all night to make love. Perhaps now they needed a release to celebrate their success, or something like that. It gave his cock permission to take over anyway.

Soon he was plunging in and out of her, each stroke bringing him closer and closer to release. She moaned and thrust back against him, her face a mixture of passion and wonder. He watched her beautiful eyes as her release hit. Her pupils widened until her eyes looked almost black, closing to half-mast as her mouth opened in a silent shout.

"Gideon!" She whispered his name as she found her pleasure. The very sound of it pushed him over the edge.

He slammed into her pussy, faster and faster as his orgasm started somewhere near his toes, traveling through him like a lightning bolt. By the time it landed between his legs, he was blind and deaf with ecstasy. Her pussy walls closed around his staff, milking him as he spilled his seed into her.

Gideon collapsed beside her, trying not to squash her with his bulk. She took his hand in hers and interlaced their fingers. Without a word, she told him so much.

Truthfully, he was scared sex with any other woman would never give him the amazing, exquisite experience he'd just had. He was already in love with her and knew he wanted to spend the rest of his life with her. How he'd accomplish that remained to be seen.

Chloe was up early, peeling herself out of the bed she had shared, for the second time, with Gideon. She had no one to blame but herself. After all, she practically invited him to be with her again. It wasn't her fault entirely—he had shown her such great pleasure, her body craved more of it. She'd never thought herself a hussy, but it took the right man to make it come to the surface.

As she pulled on the new clothes, she remembered his reaction when he saw her dressed in them. It had been such an indulgence to buy them. She'd never spent twenty dollars on anything in her life, much less clothes bought in a store. Gideon hadn't batted an eye at the cost. He just handed over money as if it were leaves on a tree.

Walking back to camp from the stream with her new finery on, nervous energy fluttered through her. The entire outfit was like a dream, something unreal although she could touch it and feel it. It probably wasn't an uncommon thing for Gideon, and she didn't want to look like a fool if she kept touching her clothes. Instead she put them on as though they weren't the most beautiful things she had owned. She had coffee started while he silently cleaned up their bed. Chloe was embarrassed enough to be unable to glance at her lover.

Lover.

The word sounded naughty, and yet it was accurate. He was her lover, nothing more, nothing less. She wasn't going to fool herself into thinking he wanted more. After all, he'd stopped her confession of love last night, thank God. She almost made a complete ass of herself, and instead made a complete hussy of herself. Neither one was something to be proud of, but at least being a hussy was familiar.

The sun painted the sky pink as they ate a silent breakfast. She shifted on the rock several times until he finally looked up at her. His gaze went down her body then back up again. In the paltry light, she couldn't quite see his expression.

"That's all you bought yesterday."

She wasn't sure if it was a question. "No, I bought two dresses, boots, a hat and underthings. You ordered, I obeyed." As soon as the words left her mouth, she wanted to grab them back and throw them in the fire.

He looked down into his coffee. "You're very prickly."

"I know." Her breath came out on a sigh. "I don't mean to be, it's just, I can't seem to stop it." God knew Granny had tried for years to soften Chloe's rough edges. She hadn't been very successful.

"You look nice." His simple compliment gave her goose bumps.

"I do?" She touched the riding skirt with her fingertips, still surprised by how velvety it was.

"Yes, you do." He looked up at her, and she swore there were sparks shooting from his blue eyes. "I knew there was a beautiful woman underneath that ugly dress."

She swallowed, her mouth as dry as dirt. "Beautiful?" No one, not even Granny, had ever told her she was beautiful, and the mirror didn't tell her any different.

"Is that hard for you to believe?"

"Yes." She picked at a piece of moss on the rock. "I know I ain't beautiful."

He scooted over until he sat beside her. She resisted the urge to blush or hide her face, although it was damn hard. He cupped her cheek, his thumb brushing across her skin.

"There are different kinds of beautiful. Sometimes you have

to look past the frosting and look at the cake."

She scowled at him. "Are you saying I'm a cake?"

He chuckled. "No, what I'm saying is, you are beautiful. Don't ever believe any different." His kiss was softer than a butterfly wing, just enough to make her breath catch and her heart skip a beat.

Chloe didn't know how to respond, so she kept her mouth shut. Gideon waited a few moments, and then he returned to his seat on the opposite side of the fire. The rest of breakfast passed in silence, but it was a more comfortable silence. Chloe allowed herself to hope for the best for the first time since her family had been taken. She saddled her horse with ease, and they packed up quickly to get started on their pursuit. Ten minutes later, Gideon broke the silence.

"I have a few things to tell you." His voice was grave, the softness he'd shown that morning completely gone.

Chloe's stomach quivered at the quietly spoken words. "What?" Her imagination took flight, finding too many awful things to fill in the unknown.

"I had a talk with the livery owner yesterday in town. He told me a man came in to get a cinch strap fixed early morning before we got into town. I got a general description, and I don't know if it's one of the men we're chasing or not. He was a stranger, there eight hours before us, and he rode in the direction we're following."

Elation swept through her. "Why didn't you tell me?"

"I figured you'd make us keep riding in the dark even when it was dangerous to do so." He sounded matter-of-fact, damn sure of himself.

"I wouldn't have."

"Yes, you would've."

"You're annoying."

"I've heard that before."

She wanted to smack him as she clenched her hands into fists. "What else haven't you told me?"

"I visited the sheriff, told him what happened. It happened out of his jurisdiction, but he's putting out a wire to local lawmen to put them on alert." He ran his hand down his whiskered cheek, the rasp loud in the quiet morning air. "By the time anyone goes looking, it might be too late to find them."

"Is that supposed to be good news?" Her anger began to bubble as he continued in his flat voice.

"No, it's not, but it's honest. I also wired my cousin, who is a lawman back in Tanger. He'll probably do more than the old sheriff in the town we just passed through." He turned to look at her. "I'm telling you this because I know finding your family is going to depend on us." His eyes glittered beneath the brim of his hat. "I bought us each a rifle and a pistol. I know you can use them, and you will likely have to."

Chloe's anger dissipated as quickly as it had come. She finally heard what he was saying.

"We're going to war."

He nodded tightly. "I can't guarantee what will happen, but I made a promise to you and I aim to keep it."

She wanted to say a thousand things, but the first thing that came to her mind was foolish. He didn't want to hear she'd fallen in love with him.

"Do you see that?"

Chloe peered ahead. Her heart leapt at the sight of the dust cloud in the distance. "Yep, I see it."

"You ready, little soldier?"

"As ready as you are, big captain." She gritted her teeth

and kneed the horse into action.

They rode side by side, streaks of horse and human in the morning light. Dust and tiny rocks pelted her face, but she ignored them. Her breath came in short gasps as they closed the distance foot by foot. She couldn't think of a better man to have beside her with her family in her sights. The sound of the horses' hooves echoed through her bones, making her feel invincible.

Soon they were close enough to actually see the back of the wagon, and Chloe growled when she recognized it. "Son of a bitch, it's them!"

Chloe leaned down farther, nearly lying on the horse's neck. She vaguely heard Gideon cursing at her, but she ignored him and pushed Lightning harder.

In a heartbeat, everything changed. The sky was above her, then the dirt, then the sky, then the dirt. She slammed into the ground hard enough to steal her breath. The last thing she heard was a horse's cry of pain before a wall of black stole over her eyes.

Gideon yanked hard on the horse's reins, his heart in his throat. He was off the horse before it stopped moving. He'd seen Chloe and her horse go down out of the corner of his eye. Her small form bounced on the packed dirt and got tangled up with the horse and the reins. Somehow Chloe had ended up with her leg underneath the horse's rump. The mare's foreleg was clearly broken, the protruding white bone glistening with blood in the morning sun, which meant there was no chance to save it. He could only hope Chloe's leg wasn't broken too.

She lay in the dust on her back, her now dirty new hat covering her face. Gideon's heart had stopped beating for a moment—everything stopped for him. He slipped out of the saddle and ran to her faster than he thought possible. When she moaned, he was able to take a breath, and then his fear slid into anger. He cursed at the foolhardy way she had surged ahead. Chloe might have broken her neck or worse to be a few seconds closer to her family.

"Damn fool thing you did, Chloe. Why did you push Lightning like that? We were catching them without your stupid tricks. Remind me of my cousin Lee, always out in front of everyone else, trying to get yourself killed."

When he knelt beside her, he was shocked to realize he was shaking. His complaints had come from his fear, not from annoyance. All those years with the Devils, many scrapes, skirmishes and outright battles, never once did he tremble with fear. Until now.

What had Chloe done to him?

He moved her hat off her face to find her grimacing in pain. "You're alive."

"I think I hurt my leg, Gid. It's paining me something awful." She tried to move, then hissed through her teeth.

Although he wanted to yell at her again, he didn't. "The mare is on your leg. I'm going to try to pull her. I think she's in more pain than you are, so this is going to be hell for both of you."

"Do it." She gritted her teeth, reminding him again of a soldier with her courage and fortitude.

He took hold of the mare's bridle, wrapping the reins around his hand. What he had to do was cruel to the horse, but he had to move her, and there was no way he could budge a thousand-pound animal alone.

"Hyah, Lightning! C'mon, girl, up, up, up!" He yanked hard on the reins, pulling at the horse as she struggled to get to her feet.

The mare screamed in pain when her broken leg hit the dirt, the sound echoing around them and in his head, but Gideon had to ignore it. It was either hurt her one last time or leave Chloe beneath her to die a slow death. His heart clenched as he tried to block out the sound of the horse's agony. Tears pricked his eyes, or maybe it was dust. He was yanking for all he was worth to move the horse, his muscles nearly ripping from the bone.

"I'm free, Gid. I'm free." Chloe had managed to scramble backward. He could see her near the brush, ten feet from the horse.

Gideon could have wept with relief as he slowly let the reins loose on the horse. Her big brown eyes rolled round as she struggled against the pain, against his hold. He drew his pistol with reluctance. He stroked her neck, whispering his thanks for her bravery, then pulled the trigger to put her out of her misery.

He used the excuse of cleaning his gun to get a grip on his runaway emotions. The last five minutes had been intense, and his blood thumped through him so hard his ears hurt. He didn't expect the hand on his back or the arms wrapped around his middle. When she pressed her face against him, he could not stop his tears. Chloe didn't judge or scoff at him, she simply held him, her own tears wetting his shirt.

Ten minutes passed before either of them moved. Chloe was in pain, but she didn't think anything was broken, mostly sore and bruised. Thank God Gideon was able to shift the horse, or Chloe may have been further injured by the mare she'd destroyed. He handed her a neckerchief, and she wiped her eyes, thankful he didn't say anything.

The sound of the horse's cries would forever echo in her mind. It was brutal, and Chloe hated the fact she was the cause. If only she hadn't spurred Lightning hard, maybe she wouldn't have broken her leg. Guilt weighed heavily on Chloe's shoulders, and she accepted it as her due.

"How did you manage to get over to me?" he asked as he pressed his face into his sleeve.

"I crawled. I hurt, but nothing's broken." She touched her leg and was pleased when she could bend all her joints. "Still hurts though."

"Can you walk?"

"I don't know. Give me a couple more minutes to sit here. I feel like I've been through a twister."

Gideon got to his feet. "We can't sit here for long, especially if you need a doctor." His eyes were red-rimmed, and his expression graver than she'd seen it before.

"I don't need a doctor." Chloe knew if Granny were there, she'd have some kind of poultice to put on her leg to take away the pain. Yet another reason not to sit any longer than necessary. They needed to keep moving. "Let's just ride double until we can get another horse."

What she didn't say was she had no idea how they would pay for the horse. Gideon had money, but she had just wasted a good deal of it by killing the mare. Her throat burned with bile and shame at what had happened. Why was it no matter what she tried, it always ended badly? Life was not kind to Chloe Ruskin.

Gideon walked around examining the horse while she sat there and felt sorry for herself. Self-pity was not a pretty thing to witness, and she didn't blame him a bit.

"It was a gopher hole."

She glanced up at him, her entire body ready to run. "A hole?"

"Yes, Chloe, a gopher hole. She snapped her foreleg." He pointed to the injury. "I've seen it plenty enough times to recognize it." He glanced at her, his intense expression a little unsettling.

"Was it my fault?"

He shook his head. "Not necessarily. She could've stepped in that hole no matter how fast you were riding."

Relief flooded through her, but the guilt remained deeply entrenched inside her heart. "She was a good horse."

"Yep, she was. Now we see just how good her partner is."

Before she could react, he scooped her into his arms and walked toward Thunder, who grazed placidly in the shade of a big cottonwood tree. She opened her mouth to protest, but shut it as the feeling of being in his arms washed over her. It felt good, more than good, it felt right. His heart beat a steady tattoo against her, his arms warm and strong. She could get used to being swept off her feet by a man like Gideon. Silly nonsense of course, but nonetheless, her mind kept wishing for it. Or was that her heart?

He set her down in the tall grass and started feeling her legs for breaks. She let him do it, although she'd already told him nothing was broken.

"Nothing's broken." He even took off her boots and checked her toes.

"Hm, that's good news." His fingers felt more than pleasant on her bare feet.

"Are you mocking me?" His frown could have cut glass.

"No, I, um, was distracted by your hands," she blurted. His expression changed.

"Oh." He took his hands away, holding them up in the air as if she was pointing a gun at him.

"I guess I won't ask you to touch me again, then." She couldn't help but feel stung by his actions. It wasn't as if they hadn't been together in the biblical sense.

"Jesus, Chloe, I didn't mean... Oh hell." He took her face and kissed her then, his lips hot and hard.

Chloe wrapped her arms around his shoulders, tugging him closer until his chest was pressed against hers. He gentled his lips then pulled away. She wanted to yank him right back.

"Now, does that feel like I don't want to touch you?" His breath was a hot burst on her skin.

Chloe's entire body screamed for more, to be naked with him in the soft, tall grass, to join with him and quench the burning desire currently thrumming through her.

"I want to touch you too."

He kissed her hard. "We don't have time for touching now. Let's get your boot back on and see if we can catch up to the wagon again."

His reminder about what they were doing was like a slap. How could she get distracted by Gideon when her family was still being held against their will? Shame crept into her cheeks as she pulled her stockings and boots on.

He held out his hand. "Let's see if you can stand."

Chloe attempted to get up, but her knee buckled and only Gideon's intervention prevented her from falling face first into the dirt.

"I don't think you can. We're going to have to go back to Westville."

"No." She tried again and again to get up, and soon her knee throbbed in agony. Chloe struggled against fury and helplessness. Her heart howled at the heavens for bringing her so close to her family, then snatching it all away.

"Yes. Don't argue with me or I will tie you to the saddle and ride back with you belly down." His expression had turned hard. "You know you need a doctor, and we know they're friendly."

Chloe couldn't quite bring herself to say yes. She just nodded and waited for him to pick her up. She stewed at the cruel twist of fate. This time his arms didn't feel as good wrapped around her.

Chapter Eight

Westville looked the same as it had the day before. Gideon rode in with a silent Chloe behind him, her anger almost palpable. He knew it wasn't directed at him, but still he could nearly see it in the air around them, shimmering in the late-day sun. They stopped at the mercantile again, this time with only one horse and one furious woman.

He dismounted carefully, leaving her on the saddle alone. When he pointed his finger at her, her nostrils flared and a muscle jumped in her cheek.

"Sit here for a few minutes. I'm going to ask the Newtons where the doctor is."

She didn't answer or even nod—she just kept staring at him from beneath her dusty hat, her expression tight.

Gideon hadn't dealt with a woman who was more stubborn than him before. It was as if she looked into his soul and determined what would drive him loco, then continued to do it every moment of every day. He would be hard-pressed to find another female within a thousand miles who could drive him more crazy.

Yet he was still not only attached to her but wanted to keep her by his side forever.

Joseph Newton was behind the counter, and his face registered surprise when he saw Gideon. "I didn't expect to see you again."

"We need a doctor for my wife. Is there anyone in town?" He prayed the friendly little town had something resembling a physician, or he'd have to ride on. It was the reason he'd ridden back here. He had no idea what lay ahead or how long it would take to get there.

"John Perkins is a vet, and he doctors people too." Joseph came around to the front. "Can I help?"

"Just tell me where Perkins is, and I'll be out of your way."

Joseph shook his head. "You are good folks. You're not in my way, and I want to help." He turned toward the back of the store. "Daisy, I'll be back in a while."

Daisy came out from behind the blue curtain. She nodded at Gideon. "Everything okay?"

"No, the Blackwoods need Doc Perkins." Joseph led the way out the door, and Gideon followed, grateful for his new friends in Westville.

Chloe sat where he'd left her, her jaw set tight enough he thought he could hear her teeth grinding. She glanced at Joseph, then back at Gideon.

"Hang on, we're going to the doctor." He took Thunder's reins and followed the shopkeeper down the street. Chloe's stare burned into his back. She would be a long time in getting over her anger. Too bad she'd have to endure the doctor's care.

If he could, he'd leave her there and ride hell for leather after the wagon with her family. However, he would break any bond they had if he left without her. She would never forgive him, and that he couldn't live with. Her anger, he would.

It took only a few minutes to walk over to the doctor's, a small yellow house with an enormous barn behind it. Joseph knocked on the door as Gideon held up his arms for Chloe. She still didn't speak, but she leaned down into him and winced only a few times as she found a comfortable spot.

"I'm sorry, little one," he whispered in her ear as he walked up the steps. She ignored him again.

The doctor answered the door right away. He had obviously been working, judging by the dirt on his clothes and the leaves in his silvery hair. His expression was assessing and guarded.

"This is Gideon and Chloe Blackwood." Joseph gestured to them. "She's hurt and needs help."

She stiffened in Gideon's arms at the introduction but remained silent.

"Her mare stepped into a gopher hole, snapped her foreleg. I don't think Chloe broke anything, but she's in pain." Gideon could only hope Doc Perkins was a competent doctor.

"Bring her in and let's have a look." He opened the door wider. "Joseph, bring them to the exam room while I clean up."

The shopkeeper led them down the narrow hallway to a room with three windows, which let in a significant amount of light. There were plenty of medical instruments around and an exam table large enough to fit any human and most small animals too.

Gideon set her down, then started removing her boots. She slapped his hand away, much to Joseph's amusement, apparently, because he stifled a laugh.

"I can take off my own boots," she snapped. "Just go away."

He didn't want to be hurt by her words, but they stung anyway. Joseph sobered, giving Gideon a sympathetic look. The two of them stepped outside the exam room as the doctor returned.

"There is a sitting room at the front of the house. You may wait there, Mr. Blackwood." Doctor Perkins shut the door in

Gideon's face.

"Friendly sort."

Joseph walked down the hall. "He doesn't have a good bedside manner, but he's a good doctor."

Gideon followed the shopkeeper, his patience worn thin. Beneath the annoyance was fear for her and for yet another delay in their journey to find her family. Chloe could truly be injured and too stubborn to admit it, although he was relieved she allowed him to go to the doctor. He'd never felt so mixed up or confused in his life.

"She'll be all right." Joseph clapped him on the shoulder. "Your wife seems like a tough lady."

Gideon's snort was part pain, part humor. "You have no idea how right you are."

"Being a husband can have its hard days." Joseph was trying to be helpful, but he only reminded Gideon that he wasn't a husband, even on a hard day. The other man went back to the store a few minutes later, leaving Gideon with his thoughts. They were all centered around Chloe. A short time passed before the doctor emerged from the exam room. His brusqueness also told Gideon the man was only doing his job, nothing more. A different kind of man than he'd met in town.

"She's bruised, maybe a light sprain, but nothing serious. A few days rest and she'll be fine." The doctor gave Gideon a slip of paper and two paper-wrapped packets. "That there is my bill along with two packets of laudanum for her. I take cash only."

Gideon stared at the scribbled writing through gritty eyes. "How much?"

"Five dollars."

It was a small fortune for just examining Chloe, but Gideon wasn't going to argue. He handed the man payment and rose to his feet. Exhaustion made him lose his balance, and he grabbed onto the doorjamb for support.

"I'm going to find the hotel then be back for my wife." He pointed at the cash in the older man's hands. "That should buy me at least another half an hour in your exam room while I find a place for her to rest."

The doctor nodded tightly then walked toward the door. "Hotel's down past the bank. Big two-story building."

With that Gideon left the doctor's house, sucking in fresh air like a tonic to cure his ails. He jumped up on Thunder and made his way down the street to the hotel. Some folks said hello, others nodded at him. Westville reminded him a bit of how Tanger was now, and a wave of homesickness hit him hard, snatching his breath.

He could scarcely believe it had less than a week since he'd left and already it felt like years. Once he returned, he wouldn't venture far again. He'd wasted time searching for where he belonged and what he was supposed to be doing with his life, and it was right there in front of him.

Now at the edge of nowhere with the bad men a fair piece ahead and a stubborn woman at his side, what he most wanted was to go home. To Tanger. He knew where he belonged now.

Chloe handed the doctor the empty glass of whatever concoction she'd just swallowed. "Where is my husband?" She frowned at the doctor, her brain a little muddled.

"I told you he was going to the hotel."

"Without me? Why would he do that?" She couldn't believe Gideon had left her there with the strange old man who smelled like horses. She hadn't been separated from Gideon since they started on their perilous journey.

"All I know is he paid me five dollars and said he would be back after he got the hotel room." The doctor stared at her without blinking.

Five dollars? Gideon paid this man five dollars to take care of her? What had he been thinking? The doctor hadn't done anything worth one dollar much less five. She thought Westville was a good place, but there was one bad apple in the barrel, that was for sure.

"How about you bring me to where he is?"

"I don't provide that kind of service to my patients. You'll have to wait until he returns." With that, the silver-haired man left. He gave her the shivers, and she was glad to see his back end leave the room.

She sat there, breathing hard, her leg still throbbing, and got madder as time ticked by. Didn't Gideon think he should tell her where he was going? He owed her the common courtesy to let her know when he was going to strand her at the creepy man's house. She didn't even have her gun or knife. Gideon had stripped it off her when they arrived and left her helpless.

She didn't like it one bit.

As soon as she heard his familiar tread in the hallway, her fear began to fade, and her annoyance intensified. He poked his head in and she started on him before he even had a chance to get in the room.

"How dare you leave me here, Gid?" Instead of roaring at him, her words came out soft, ending on a pitiful note that made her cringe.

"Ah, honey, I didn't leave you." He scooped her up and walked out of the doctor's house. "I was just looking for a place to rest our heads tonight."

She wanted to be angry but found she was more hurt instead. Of course that just made her angry all over again. It was a tug-of-war with her emotions, and she lost no matter what happened. Gideon had turned her into a simpering idiot.

He slipped her up onto the saddle, then mounted behind her. His strong arms surrounded her as the gentle rocking of the horse soothed her. It was comfortable, familiar, perfect. She could get used to being there easily. She belonged with him, feeling his heart beat and his warm breath on her neck. What had the doctor given her? She was a little light-headed and definitely sleepy.

"The doctor made me drink something." She could hardly understand herself.

"Probably laudanum for the pain and to relax you. Don't worry, Chloe, I won't let anything happen to you." His voice sounded far away.

"I'm mad at you." She tried to focus on his face, but it was so hard she closed her eyes instead.

"I know you are."

The horse stopped, and she nearly fell out of the saddle. He gripped her tightly.

"Now I've got to get you down without breaking your leg or my head."

Chloe kept breathing in his scent, the familiarity making her feel safe. She opened her eyes long enough to see him contorting himself into an awkward position with one foot on the ground, the other half on the saddle. It would have been funny if she could laugh, but her mouth didn't work right.

He must've found his balance, because soon she was in his arms again as he carried her up a flight of stairs. Flowery wallpaper followed her up.

"Di' I fall ashleep?" Chloe's tongue had decided not to work either.

"Yes, you did. Just sleep, honey, I've got you."

The feeling of warmth, safety and love washed over her as she snuggled into the soft bed beneath her. Even her leg didn't hurt anymore. Best of all, she could still smell Gideon and knew he was there, just as he'd promised.

After taking care of the horse and grabbing their gear, he went back to the room to find Chloe fast asleep. He had no idea how much laudanum the doctor had given her, but it was enough to knock her on her ass. Gideon stared down at her as she slept like an angel. It apparently took a dose of a heavy drug to make her sleep that way, but they both needed the rest. Being with her put him on edge, or maybe it was his own reaction to her. The last few days had felt like a year with all the shenanigans and almost unbelievable happenings.

He sat on the chair in the corner, and the wood complained about his weight. There was no way he was going to able to sleep on it, which meant either the floor or the bed. His obvious choice was the bed, but that meant being in close proximity to Chloe all night. That might hinder his ability to sleep at all. However, he couldn't stay in the chair.

He crept over to the bed, then climbed in beside her on top of the blanket. As she snored softly, he watched her sleep. There was less than ten years between their ages, but he felt much older, more bitter about life. Chloe was full of righteousness and didn't ever stop to think about what she was doing, only that she knew it was the right choice.

Is that what he'd been missing? The hunger for life, for doing what was right and for living life rather than existing? He had been guilty of hanging on to the past, for not following the path laid out in front of him. He was afraid of the unknown, of becoming the man he could be. As a spoiled boy and young man, he'd done nothing of consequence. As an army captain, he'd led his men and survived the war with them. As just a man with nothing but his friends, he had struggled against himself. It almost seemed pitiful to think about it now.

The past was past, and his stubbornness kept him from moving on. It took a stubborn, outspoken, alluring, curly-haired loco woman to drag him from the ditch he'd been hiding in. He brushed the hair back from her face, then leaned down and kissed her cheek.

As he lay down beside her, he had the sudden realization it was the first time in his life he was going to sleep all night in bed with a woman.

The sun streamed through the windows, filling the room with bright light. Chloe felt like someone had stuck a wet sock in her mouth. She tried to swallow but couldn't muster up enough spit to do it. A heavy weight lay across her waist, and someone snored in her ear. It took her a few more seconds to recognize Gideon.

She was in a bed. With Gideon. In a strange room.

What the hell had happened?

She searched her memory and found a smattering of images from the day before. The horse, her leg, a grumpy doctor, then nothing. She didn't even remember the room, much less agreeing to sleep in a bed with him. Not much different than a bedroll, but it was a *bed*. That was what a husband and wife did, not two strangers who happened to collide in the middle of nowhere, their fates entwined by cruel reality.

The doctor had given her some kind of medicine to make her sleep. She didn't usually cotton to taking anything, but she'd been in too much pain to protest at the time. It was a damn dirty trick he'd played on her, and she had a feeling she knew who was behind it.

"Get off me, Blackwood." She pushed at his arm, surprised by how heavy he was when he was dead asleep. "I said, get off me!" This time she shouted at him, her voice echoing in the room, bouncing off the bright white walls.

He was up in an instant, gun in hand, shirt off. She stared at the wide expanse of chest, the whorls of hair around his flat nipples that led down his stomach to his manly parts. A pink scar stood out on his side, a new one, judging by the look of it. Other scars peppered his skin here and there, but they were years old and whitened by age. Holy God, the man's beauty made her entire body clench. If she wasn't so mad at him, she'd ask him to bed her.

"You tricked me."

He set the gun down gently onto the chair in the corner. "I did no such thing."

"You gave me something to make me sleep."

"No, the doctor did. I just carried you here." He ran his hand down his face. "Jesus, woman, you sure know how to wake up a man."

She looked at his trousers, and Lord have mercy, his cock was clearly hard as it strained against the fabric. Her body heated, growing wet with need. She tried to shove away the arousal, but it was insistent and powerful. Her frustration overwhelmed her, and her temper let loose.

"I can't believe I let myself do this. Granny should have stopped me." She shook her finger at him. "You were not the man to give myself to for my first time! You're a devil of a man, and I regret the day I crawled into the wagon."

"What?" His brows slammed together. "What did you say?"

"You heard me. I shouldn't have done what I did. It's only caused me trouble and strife since I lay with a man, with you! I could have gone to my grave without knowing how it changed a person to be with a man." She pointed at his crotch. "That truly is a one-eyed snake, and I wish I'd never known what pleasure it brings." Chloe stood with some difficulty, her knee screaming in protest. She faced him with her hands on her hips, wearing only her brand-new chemise and a hefty scowl. "I can't even look at you without wanting to tussle in the sheets with you."

In seconds, his expression changed from shock to sizzling anger. She realized too late what she had blurted out. Damn sure couldn't shove the words back into her fool mouth. Oh boy, she had stepped in a pile of horse shit for sure.

"What was that you just told me?" He stepped toward her, and she took a step back. "Did you just tell me your *grandmother* knew you bedded me?"

His voice made her ears hurt, so she clapped her hands over them.

"Oh no, you will hear what I have to say."

"The folks at the mercantile can hear what you have to say." She looked around for an escape but found none. He blocked the door with his bulk.

"Not funny, Chloe. Not funny in the least." He loomed over her. "You tricked me. You and your cackling granny tricked me. I can't believe I was about to..." His eyes narrowed. "Did you just tell me you were a virgin before we met?"

"No, I never said that." Oh hell, she hadn't meant to let that slip.

"Not exactly those words, but you just told me I was the first man you'd lain with." He tugged at his hair as his face registered a hundred different emotions. "I can't believe you did that. Jesus, Chloe, I thought I was, I mean, that we had something. It was all a lie. One big fat lie."

She couldn't deny it. Heck, she didn't even have an excuse. Granny convincing her to follow her instincts wasn't a very strong reason. Chloe could have not gone through with it, but she had. No, she'd gone ahead and done exactly what he accused her of—seducing him because she wanted to. Then again, it had been the right thing to do, no matter the consequences. She'd never known what it meant to be close to another person, to experience such joy and pleasure in his arms.

"It wasn't all a lie." She did feel real things for Gideon, emotions she didn't even know she had.

"What part?" He paced back and forth, looking angrier by the second. "What part wasn't a lie?" Gideon leaned toward her, his nostrils flaring, his eyes full of fury and pain.

Her hand shook as she reached up to touch him. He jerked back, pulling her heart right along with him. Agony radiated out from her chest, dragging her down into the depths of misery. Chloe could hardly get in a breath as she told herself not to cry.

"What part, Chloe?"

"I-I like you." It was such a silly thing to say, not even true either. She did more than like him.

He snorted. "Does that excuse what you did? Chloe, I took your virginity. Do you know what that means? It means you just got yourself a husband. A real one this time."

She stared at him, her mouth open as his words settled in her brain. "Husband?"

"I don't make it a habit of bedding virgins. If I had, I'd have been married by now." Gideon leaned in until they were nearly touching noses. "You will marry me."

It was what she wanted. Her heart did a funny jig at the

thought, but when she opened her mouth, something else entirely happened.

"No."

If she'd thought he looked surprised before, it was nothing compared to his expression now.

"Did you just say no?"

"Yep, I said no. I ain't marrying you because you think you have to." She shook her head even as her heart cracked, and she knew he was slipping through her fingers. "No husband that's forced is gonna ever love his wife."

Gideon's harsh breathing filled the room as he stared at her. She held her ground, unwilling to be shackled to a man who felt obligated to make her his wife. Chloe never expected to marry for love, but she would not marry because of a man's guilt.

"I can't believe you said no."

"Well, believe it because I said no. We need to get moving since we wasted the whole night here in this town." She sat on the side of the bed, trying to ignore him.

"The doctor said you have to rest a couple of days." He stood over her, attempting to intimidate her with his size.

"I don't care what the damn doctor said. I'm leaving whether or not you like it." Her knee was sore, hell, her whole body hurt, but she had gotten up on both feet. She'd work out the kinks and be right as rain in no time. The doctor was a fool.

"A horse fell on you yesterday, Chloe. You need to recover." He put his hand on her arm.

She shook it off. "I need to find my family. You can either help me or get out of my way." Chloe wanted to hit him, push him, get him out of her line of vision. If she didn't, she might do something stupid like tell him she changed her mind about marrying him. His scent surrounded her and she could hardly think straight for being distracted by this intense, intelligent man who had changed her life.

"I don't think it's a good idea." He frowned at her as she hobbled across the room. It took great effort not to show him how difficult it actually was.

"Good thing you don't have to think about it, then. It's my decision, Blackwood." She managed to pull on her dusty clothes, wishing she had time to at least brush off the dirt. No time to worry about vanity—pursuing her family was more important.

"You are an infuriating woman." He was gritting his teeth hard enough she thought she saw sparks coming from his mouth.

"I don't even know what that word means." She sucked in a breath as the skirt slid up her bruised thigh. Closing her eyes, she pictured the girls and Granny and ignored the pain as best she could.

He fussed like an old woman as she finished dressing, hovering behind her and huffing. She was nearly ready to run away, pain and all. Heading for the door, she saw her neatly stacked belongings. The sight stopped her in her tracks. He'd taken care of her and their things. He truly was a good man, and he had offered to marry her, which meant he was an honorable man.

Chloe knew she owed him her life and a good deal of respect. He could have left her days ago, but he didn't. She sighed from the bottom of her toes, then decided to do the right thing even if she didn't want to. "Will you carry our things downstairs?"

"You're crazy." He sounded angry, but he still picked up their things and opened the door. "I am only doing this because

I know you will leave without me. You're a stubborn woman, Chloe Ruskin."

"I reckon I've heard that a time or two." She did not want to talk about her faults, however plentiful they were. "Let's get a move on."

She made her way out the door and to the top of the stairs. There was nothing to hang on to, just an open set of stairs to the lobby. She leaned against the wall and stepped down slowly as if she were a toddler learning to use her feet. Gideon pushed past her, set their things on the floor below, then came bounding back up the stairs two at a time.

"You are going to send me to an early grave." He picked her up and carried her the rest of the way down the stairs.

Chloe was grateful he'd done it, but she wouldn't tell him that. It would give him too much satisfaction.

"I could've made it."

He snorted. "Not if you wanted to leave today."

"Hmph. You're turning into a bully again."

"I'm trying to take control of our situation because right now it's a rogue cannonball and I have no idea where it's going to hit next." He set her gently onto a wooden chair in the corner, then piled their things on the floor beside her. "Now sit here while I go see about getting you a new horse."

She wanted to tell him to stop being bossy and ask her instead of telling her, but he was out the door before she could.

"Your husband is a patient man." The desk clerk couldn't have been more than eighteen, with wide dark eyes and floppy brown hair. He stared after Gideon as if he'd seen the second coming of Jesus.

"And you're an idiot." She ignored his gasp and focused on the door, willing Gideon to come back so they could leave

Westville.

Her family was waiting for her to save them, and she couldn't let them down.

Gideon had to stop himself halfway to the livery when he realized he was actually stomping down the road. Stomping! Chloe had reduced him to this, a babbling man acting like a spoiled child. He never stomped or was impolite to women or slept with virgins either.

That last thought gave him pause, and he had to literally force himself to breathe a few times. He'd been right to want to marry her, and the fact he'd been her first made him that much more determined to become her husband. Who would have thought a trip to Nate's would land him in the middle of nowhere with an unwilling bride and some nasty kidnappers to chase?

If it wasn't true, it might even have been funny.

Frank was waiting for him in the doorway of the stable. The big old German had his arms crossed and a frown on his face.

"I heard you came back into town. What happened to my horses?"

Gideon considered telling the man to go to hell but thought better of that choice. He was the only man in the small town with horses to buy. "Lightning hit a gopher hole and snapped her foreleg. I had to put her down."

Frank closed his eyes. "I raised that horse from a filly."

Gideon finally understood what Frank was upset about and felt bad he'd been the one to end the horse's life. "She was a good horse."

"She was the last I had from her dam, a mare my father gave me when I was a boy." Frank sighed and wiped his eyes with grimy hands. "I suppose you're going to be needing another horse for your wife."

"If you have one. She's not going to sit still for long." Gideon didn't have much money left, but he had the letter of credit from the bank. "I can go down and get the money, but it'd be easier to write you a voucher to cash at the bank."

Frank turned and walked into the stable. "I've got one more mare that might be the right one."

Gideon followed him, again grateful for the good folks of Westville. He'd never needed friends more.

Chapter Nine

Chloe thought she'd stare a hole through the door of the hotel waiting for Gideon to return. She couldn't get far by walking, that was for sure. The clerk kept watching her with his piggy eyes. If she wasn't alone and unable to run, she would have given him a piece of her mind for acting like an ass. Helpless was not an easy state for her to accept.

When the door opened and Gideon walked in, her traitorous heart did a little pitty-pat, then a somersault. The man ought not to look so good, bound to give a lovesick fool like her a fit of the vapors to catch a glimpse of him. He even had a basket on his arm that smelled a lot like biscuits. "I've got food for the trail. Frank had another mare. If you're ready, we can go."

If she was ready? She hadn't wanted to even come to Westville, much less be drugged and spend the night. He had done it because she was injured, but the deception by the doctor and Gideon still stuck in her craw.

"I was ready yesterday."

He ignored her barb and scooped her up in his arms, his strength surprising her again. They emerged onto the street, and she shaded her eyes against the sun, then her breath caught. Standing there saddled and ready was the most beautiful paint she'd ever seen. Milky white with warm dark brown spots.

"She's beautiful."

"That she is. Frank charged me twice what she was worth." Gideon helped her into the saddle gently, taking care to put her foot in the stirrup so slowly she almost kicked him to hurry up.

"I'm not going to break, you know."

His head snapped up, and she saw more than annoyance in his expression—she saw hurt. Through all her anger and self-pity, she'd hurt him. Big, strong man that he was, Gideon had feelings just like everyone else.

"I'm sorry," she blurted.

"Done is done, Chloe. Let me go get our things and we'll be on our way." He walked away, taking her heart with him.

They set off at a much slower pace. Gideon refused to go any faster and once threatened to hold the reins of the paint, who was named Bella, until she stopped complaining about how fast they weren't going.

Even through her complaints about the pace, Chloe was very sore, and every bump on the trail reverberated through her. After an hour she was grateful he had insisted on such a pace. If she'd been trotting or, God forbid, galloping, she would be crying in pain. As it was, she was uncomfortable, but it wasn't unbearable. She could rest later, after they found her family.

The silence between them bordered on uncomfortable, and she shouldered most of the blame. She needed to apologize to him, not yell then blurt a hurried sorry. Chloe knew she should have said yes to Gideon's marriage proposal, but her pride had stopped her. That particular fault usually muddied the waters, as much as she wanted to overcome it.

"I came from nothing, you know."

He didn't turn to look at her. "I know."

"You had tutors and money and you talk fancy. My daddy could've been one of your daddy's sharecroppers." She wanted him to see why they shouldn't marry. "We ain't from the same social circles."

His laugh was more of a rusty, painful sound. "Social circles? Hell, Chloe, I don't think there are any more of those." He shook his head. "Just because I grew up in a different type of house doesn't mean we're different in here." His fist pressed against his chest.

He was right, and she knew it, but she held on stubbornly to the idea they were too different. "You talk better, you're smarter and you're sure richer than me."

"I'm not rich, Chloe. I own part of a restaurant, and I've saved some money, that's all." He finally turned to look at her, and she saw naked longing in his expression. "Money is nothing. Love is what's important."

She couldn't look away, couldn't catch her breath. "What do you mean?"

"I fell in love with you sometime in the last few days, and I'll be damned if I can stop how I feel. You're infuriating, annoying, stubborn and the most beautiful creature I've ever laid eyes on." His jaw tightened with what looked like anger. Odd for a man who'd just told her he loved her.

He loved her.

The silence hung between them, heavy and full of unsaid emotions. It was her turn to speak, her turn to blurt her feelings for him, but she couldn't make her mouth work and her tongue ceased responding to her. Her heart nearly cracked when he looked away.

This time the silence wasn't uncomfortable. It was painful.

The sun set behind them, illuminating the trees and brush in shades of orange and pink. Gideon hadn't spent such a miserable day on a horse in years. He was in tatters, both emotionally and physically. Chloe had worn him down to a pitiful nub in need of a love he'd obviously never receive.

Zeke would've punched him.

Heck, he could've punched himself for being pathetic. It was high time he forgot about Chloe and her strange notions and focused on getting her reunited with her family so he could escape. Gideon squared his shoulders, shaking off the cloak of sadness he'd been carrying.

If Chloe didn't want to marry him, that was that. He wouldn't push her anymore, and he sure as hell wouldn't get lost in the emotional tangle with her any longer.

As if he was finally seeing clearly again, he spotted something on a bush on the side of the road. It looked a lot like a ribbon.

"Chloe, look there to the right. Is that a ribbon?"

She peered at the bush. "It looks like it. If I could get off this horse, I'd go look myself." She shifted and hissed through her teeth.

Gideon needed to find out exactly how much pain she was in, but that would have to wait until later. He rode over and dismounted in front of the bush. To his delight, it was a scrap of blue ribbon again. Despite his own situation, the sight of it made him smile.

He held it up for Chloe to see. She whooped loudly, startling a few birds from the trees, and a squirrel chattered at her. That small piece of ribbon healed whatever rift had opened between them. Or perhaps since they'd picked up the scent of their quarry, it allowed them to set aside their problematic relationship for now.

Of course eventually they'd have to deal with the fact he'd said he loved her. Of all the things to say, it wasn't what he expected to come hurtling out of his mouth.

Although he fought with his inner turmoil, they rode onward, scanning the bushes for any more clues. Chloe made small noises the longer they traveled. He didn't push her to stop, because he knew she'd refuse. The woman would probably ride with a broken leg and a bullet hole if it meant she'd be two feet closer to her family. He called a halt when it grew too dark to see anything, and for once she didn't argue.

After setting the bedrolls down, Gideon carefully picked her up from the saddle, and she moaned softly.

"That's not the kind of noise I want to hear now."

Her laugh ended on a gasp. "Just set me down, you big oaf." She bit her lip hard, and he thought he saw blood, but it was too dark to tell.

"I'm going to start a fire, then get some coffee brewing."

"Sounds mighty nice." Her voice was surprisingly weak.

Gideon gathered wood for a fire and got a blaze going in the inky darkness. After he poured water from a canteen into the pot, he threw in coffee beans and set it on the fire to boil. He returned to check on Chloe. She lay on her back, staring at the stars. He knelt beside her and cupped her cheek.

"I think you're tougher than any soldier I ever met."

"Is that a compliment? Or should I be insulted you compared me to a man?" She sighed against his hand. "Is the coffee ready yet?"

"Pushy wench." He held up the canteen. "Water?"

"No, I need something a little stronger."

"Fair enough." He tucked the blanket around her, thankful

she couldn't see him blush at the way he took care of her. When had he turned into such a coddler?

After a meager dinner of biscuits and coffee, she fell asleep still wearing her boots. Gideon made her comfortable, then spooned up behind her. He fell asleep almost as soon as he closed his eyes, holding Chloe to his heart.

Chloe woke cocooned in Gideon's warmth, his arm wrapped around her stomach. For a few precious seconds, she held on to the feeling. The moment was perfect, and then she tried to shift a tiny bit closer and the pain hit her. Stars swam in front of her eyes as she struggled not to cry out. Her knee throbbed in tune with her racing heart, although it wasn't the reason she wanted it to be racing. She must have made some kind of noise, because Gideon was awake in an instant.

"What's wrong?"

She shook her head, unable to even speak.

He flung back the bedroll and glanced down at her knee. His expression told her what she wanted to, or didn't want to, know. His lips compressed as he continued to stare; then, when he looked back at her, it was as if he was yelling at her with his eyes.

"We're going to have to get the swelling down, or you aren't riding anywhere."

Chloe should've protested, but for the first time since she'd been injured, she agreed with him. Her knee felt three times its normal size and hurt something powerful.

"I hear water nearby. I'll be back shortly." With a quick, hard kiss, he rose, shirtless. If she hadn't been in agony, she would have appreciated seeing him half-naked again. Her fingers itched to touch the whorls of dark hair, the warm skin stretched across taut muscle and bone.

He yanked on his boots, then ran into the woods beyond. She had a moment to admire his form before he disappeared from view. Chloe rolled on her back and tried to bend her knees. One worked just fine, although it was sore, the other refused to bend. That would make it mighty hard to walk, much less ride.

She managed to sit up, although sweat rolled down her skin by the time she got there. Who knew such a simple thing would be such a big chore? She pulled back the blanket to get a good look at her knee, which was a rainbow of colors from an angry purple, to green and blue. The swelling was there, but it wasn't as large as it felt. She touched the edges, and her fingers left an impression.

Chloe wondered if she should panic now.

"What are you doing?" Gideon reappeared out of nowhere and knelt beside her, his brow furrowed. "Were you going to try to walk?"

She snorted at the thought. "Not hardly. I was taking a gander at what's paining me."

He didn't look as though he entirely believed her. "I found a creek about a hundred yards away. The water is cold enough it must be fed by some hills with snow runoff." He put his arms under her knees. "This may hurt a little."

She closed her eyes against the pain as her legs hung from the knee down from his arm. She'd felt worse than this before, but it was bearable, but only just. If Gideon wasn't there holding her, she didn't think she would be doing as well.

The sound of the water grew louder as he walked, slow as molasses, of course. He stopped, and she opened her eyes. The creek was about eight feet across, with gently rolling rich green banks flanking the stream. It was a little slice of heaven. The sun was just starting to rise, painting a pinkish glow on the surface of the water.

He set her on the grass and glanced at her. "You know I never... Never mind." He fingered the leather of her skirt. "This really is good quality."

Chloe didn't know what he was doing or what was happening, and that made her nervous. She was about to open her mouth and say something terrible when he reached for her buttons. Now she just watched, as if it wasn't her he was undressing. She had always been responsible for taking care of others, and now Gideon was showing her what it meant to have someone else take care of her. It was an eye-opening experience, and as she watched him undress, with his chocolate curls a breath away, she recognized what she was feeling was love. She truly did love Gideon.

He was the man for her, and now that she had stupidly said no to his proposal, she changed her mind. However, she was too proud to tell him that and decided to wait until he asked her again. If he asked her again.

What an incredibly foolish decision in a sea of foolish decisions.

Instead of telling him how she felt, she just sat back and allowed him to take off every stitch of her clothing until she was buck naked on that grass. She wanted to cover her exposed tits with her arm, but he distracted her when he stood up.

Not only did he have a very prominent erection in his trousers, but he started taking off the rest of his clothes too. Chloe had wanted this moment since she had seen him that first time walking around their wagon with his broad shoulders, blue eyes and soft-as-feathers curls. Now he undressed in front of her, showing her exactly what she'd refused. She forgot all about her knee and the pain as he revealed his body.

His cock had always seemed large to her, but as it sprang

free from the confines of his trousers, it looked enormous. It pulsed with its own energy, standing proudly in a nest of dark curls surrounding his balls. They were large too, but not overly so. His erection twitched when he noticed her stare.

Her hand shook with the need to touch him, to feel his satin-coated steel. As she reached out, he closed his eyes. Her fingers grazed up and down his staff, which was soft and hard at the same time, such an amazing combination. Then she shifted her weight, and pain ripped through her.

Gideon immediately dropped to his knees and gently took her into his arms. He murmured apologies while he held her close.

"I'm sorry." He sounded as if he was the one in pain.

"I did the touching, not you." Chloe blew out a breath. "I can't seem to help myself around you is all."

With a strangled chuckle, he kissed her forehead. "Now let's try that cold water."

Chloe had taken cold baths, even washed up in mountain streams, but nothing prepared her for just how frigid that creek was. It was like liquid snow washing over her. She gasped as her feet sank into it, then her lower legs.

She nearly ran for shore when her pussy and behind were submerged. Every inch of skin turned into a giant goose bump. She shivered as Gideon made sure her legs were under the water.

"You don't need to worry about my stick anymore. It's now a twig." His teeth were gritted as he carried her into the deeper current.

"Cold water makes your cock shrivel?"

He snorted. "You are brash, Chloe. Yes, it shrivels up."

She stuck her hand down between them and tried to touch

him while he was small.

"What are you doing?"

"I want to feel."

"There are better times to feel, ah, me." He twitched when her hand closed around the much-smaller dick.

"It still moves when I touch it." She squeezed gently, and it responded by growing larger.

"It will always move when you touch it."

"It's getting bigger." Sure enough with each stroke, he grew larger.

He closed his eyes and stopped walking. "That's because it likes your touch."

She was fascinated by his member, different from the triangle between her legs, but made to fit together. He pulsed in her hand, and she tugged a bit harder to see what happened.

"Does that feel good? I'm not hurting you, am I?"

H shook his head. "No, honey, it's far from pain. It feels too good."

"I like to touch you."

"Thank God for that." He gestured to her knee. "How does it feel?"

"Better." She bent it a little. "The cold water is working."

"On some things." He tried to pull her hand away from his dick, but she held fast, unwilling to give him up just yet. "What are you doing, Chloe?"

"Making you feel good." She laid her head back so her hair floated on the water, then closed her eyes. Her hand continued to pleasure him.

To her delight, his hand crept between her legs. The rush of cold water was replaced by his calloused fingers. He slipped one inside her, while his thumb made slow circles on that amazingly sensitive nubbin of flesh.

"Oh, that feels good, Gid." She didn't know if normal folks did this kind of thing, but darned if it wasn't naughty and nice at the same time.

"Uh-huh." He started rocking with her movements, his staff pushing against her hand.

She opened her legs even wider, eager for more. He added a second finger, and a shiver of pure pleasure skidded across her skin. To think a week ago she had no idea what folks did under the sheets. To her, it was a cock in a pussy and that was all. Boy was she wrong. There was much more.

Her nipples ached in the cold water, needing his touch, but the position she was in would not allow him to reach her. Chloe wasn't sure how to do it, but she needed to join with him and not just play with him. She opened her eyes and peered at his face, awash in the moment of ecstasy they were sharing.

"Gideon, I need you."

"You've got me, little one." His voice sounded a bit strained, and she knew he was feeling the same goodness she was.

"No, I need your cock in my pussy. Now."

His eyes opened wide. "You will never stop surprising me."

"I don't know if that means yes or no." She squirmed against him until he let her legs float in the water.

"Yes, always yes." He pulled at her hips until she settled her legs on either side of him. His staff brushed against her, and a tiny moan popped out of her mouth.

"Good, because I need you." Her body throbbed, craving his like she never imagined. He positioned himself and slid into her in one quick thrust.

Chloe's shout echoed in the forest around them, scaring a

few birds from their roosts. She didn't care. This, *this* was where she belonged. In his arms, joined with him.

He gripped her hips as he thrust into her again and again. Their heat and friction created a fire within her that was burning her up.

She cupped her breasts and pinched them, tugging at the nipples the way he did. It was titillating and naughty. He grinned wickedly and watched each flick of her fingers. As the sensation traveled through her, her pussy clenched around him.

"God, you're tight. So fucking tight." His fingers dug into her behind. "I'm not going to be able to hold back, Chloe. Touch yourself for me. Make yourself come."

Chloe could barely put two thoughts together, but she understood what he was asking her. She'd done it before, but never with anyone and certainly not while having sex. However, the idea excited her more than she was going to admit.

Her hand crept down until she felt where they were joined. She touched the crisp hairs around his cock that tickled her fingers, then into her own moistness.

"That's it, honey." He pinched her nipple, and she grunted at the rush of pleasure.

Her fingers found the nubbin of pleasure and made clumsy circles around it. Soon she found her rhythm and realized Gideon had been right. His cock, her fingers and his hands sent her over a precipice so deep she thought it would never end.

The waves of pleasure washed over her as she climbed higher, screaming his name and pulling him deep into her core. He followed within seconds, his warm seed filling her.

His love completing her.

The cold water had revived him, while the amazing feeling of being in her arms fulfilled him. As he'd taken care of Chloe, peace had stolen over him. He had spent a good deal of time taking responsibility for others out of duty, but this time, love compelled him to. Being with her reminded him of what it meant to truly give to someone else.

Chloe didn't complain about sitting while he broke camp after a quick breakfast. He had the horses saddled and ready in ten minutes, and then he squatted in front of her. She smiled shyly, and his heart did a funny flip.

"How are you feeling?"

"Good." She glanced down at her hands on her lap. "Really good."

He grinned, his heart light and his body sated. "Ready to ride?"

When he picked her up, a jolt went through his arms, startling him bad enough he almost dropped her. She stared at him, her eyes wide, and he realized she had felt it too.

"What was that?"

"I have no idea." He looked into her green eyes and saw himself staring back. God knew he had no idea what it was about this woman that turned him inside out, but he was smart enough to accept the inevitable. "But I hope it happens again."

Chloe laughed, more of a giggle, and he was nearly as shocked as when he'd experienced the jolt.

"That's the first time I've heard you laugh."

For whatever reason, his statement made her laugh again.

"You need to do that more often."

He kissed her and stepped over to the waiting horses. After making sure she was secure in the saddle, they left the camp. Their time there had been almost magical, as though someone or something had led them there, gave them a chance to find peace and perhaps to accept the love they had for each other.

As soon as they turned and the idyllic retreat was behind them, the mood darkened. The reason they rode was too serious to maintain the playfulness they'd found in their private time together. However, the time with Chloe helped Gideon get back the focus he needed.

The day passed by quickly as they alternated between a trot and a walk. He didn't want to push Chloe too hard, but he also understood her urgency. His gut told him they were closing in on the wagon again, mostly due to the fact they were on horseback. They were making better time than when they'd been in the peddler's wagon towed by two old nags.

They even ate on horseback, Chloe refusing to stop. He noted the lines of pain around her mouth. Yet she clenched her teeth and had sheer determination in her eyes. She simply wouldn't give up until they couldn't go on.

The darkness settled over them, the stars twinkling above, and Gideon knew it was time to call a halt. Even he was tired, and he didn't have a sore knee to contend with.

"Chloe, we're stopping."

"I can still see, Gid. Let's go a little bit farther."

He reached out and grabbed her reins. "No, we're not going to risk our horses or our lives to go half a mile farther. We covered a lot of miles today already."

"But—"

"No, this time I'm going to say no, and you can't bully me into changing my mind." He steered the horses toward a flat spot near the woods they could use as a campsite.

"I don't bully you."

He snorted. "Yes, you do, but it's part of your charm. Now

shut up and let me be the man here."

"Gideon," she whispered. "Look there, through the trees."

He turned and peered into the pitch-black forest. At first he saw nothing out of the ordinary, but then he spotted it.

The orange glow of a campfire.

"It's them."

"We don't know it's them," Gideon whispered back.

"I can feel it inside. It's them." She tried to grab the reins from him. "Let me go. We're so close. I ain't gonna let them spend another night with those bastards."

Anguish filled her voice and washed across his heart. Her family could be close enough to rescue, and she was sitting there doing nothing. He'd be feeling her pain and frustration if it was his family.

"I'll walk over there. They'll hear the horses." He plucked her off the saddle and set her on a fallen log. "You sit here and watch the horses. I can't be worried about you, or I won't be any good." He secured the horses' reins to a tree, then checked his weapons.

"You'll be worried about me?" She sounded full of wonder.

"Of course I will. For God's sake, woman, I've been in love with you since the moment you pointed that pistol at my chest." He kissed her hard and trotted off into the woods.

Probably shouldn't have told her he loved her again, but if he didn't come back, at least he'd go to his maker knowing he hadn't left it unsaid. The darkness of the woods closed around him as he made his way toward the fire.

When he was close to the target, he crouched and crept along, careful to avoid any leaves or sticks to give away his position. He stopped and listened, trying to gauge who was out there. He heard the murmur of voices—two males—but no women and no children.

That didn't mean it wasn't the Ruskin wagon though. He made his way closer, inch by inch, until he was flat on his belly behind a tree, peering at the occupants of the campsite. He controlled his breathing and his heart before he ventured to look around the tree.

Two men sat on either side of the fire, both no older than he was. They each wore tattered grey pants, which he recognized well, and a pistol. Beside one was a rifle, while the other had a large knife strapped to his back. They weren't big men but were obviously well armed and expecting trouble. One had scraggly black hair, the other greasy, wavy hair, perhaps brown, and he had pockmark scars on his face. The second man appeared to be the one Frank had seen in Westville.

Gideon memorized their gear and where they kept it before his gaze moved on. His heart leapt into his throat when he spotted a bound and gagged Granny tied to one of the wagon wheels.

Holy shit. They'd found the missing Ruskins.

"Adam, there any water left?" one man asked the other.

"I ain't got no idea. Why don't you go look?" The man with his back to Gideon, who was apparently named Adam, flipped his hand toward the wagon.

The first one barely glanced that way, not even stopping to look at Granny. "Rufus, bring some water out here."

A third man poked his head out from the wagon. A rangy beard wound its way around his large face, framing a pair of close-set eyes that were more like piss holes in the snow. He looked dangerous and unpredictable. Gideon hadn't expected a third man, and this one was not only fierce-looking but was a big bastard.

"Get it yourself, you lazy son of a bitch. I ain't your slave."

"Ain't no more slaves," Adam drawled. "That bastard took 'em away."

"I'm thirsty. Bring some water out here now." The first man rose, and although he was about as tall as Gideon, his pants hung on his frame, held up by a piece of rope. Obviously the men had not been eating well for quite some time. "Or I'll shoot you." He drew his pistol with surprising speed.

Gideon wondered who these three men were and why they chose to steal the Ruskin wagon, complete with an old woman and two little girls. At least he hoped the girls were in the wagon. Since he couldn't see them, he could only hope they were safely tucked away inside.

"Put that away, Tobias. You ain't shooting nobody. Sit down," Adam ordered with an edge to his voice. "Rufus, bring the fucking water. Now."

It was apparent who the leader of the group was, and he had steel in his voice that made the hairs on Gideon's neck rise. Both of the other men obeyed the orders. Something they'd said echoed in Gideon's head.

Tobias. Adam.

Tobias. Adam.

Dear God. Chloe's brother was named Adam and her cousin was named Tobias. His heart, which had been calm with a slow, steady rhythm, now hammered against his ribs. Her family had kidnapped Granny and the girls, leaving Chloe alone to fend for herself.

How was he going to tell her?

Chloe thought she might actually explode. Not only had he ordered her to sit there while he went off to rescue her family, but he'd had the nerve to say he loved her before he disappeared into the woods. She wanted to punch him and at the same time kiss him. He was making her heart flip sideways.

After their amazing night in the creek and by the fire, she thought perhaps she had gained control of her reaction to him. Ha! She couldn't have been more wrong. It was about fifteen minutes of near torture before he ran back. She recognized his shape in the shadows, and a breath of relief gushed out of her.

Not that she'd tell him that.

"Chloe?"

"I'm here. Waiting." She managed to sound annoyed even though she whispered.

He sat beside her, his chest heaving. "I ran as fast and as quietly as I could. You could be a little nicer to me."

She wanted to shake him. "What did you see?"

Gideon blew out a breath, while Chloe could hardly catch hers.

"What did you see?" she repeated.

"What does your brother look like?"

Chloe's mouth went dry as cotton. Her heart flipped upside down, then back again. "Why?"

"Just tell me."

"I don't want to hate you, Blackwood. You'd better be sure you're asking the right question." She wanted to put her hands over her ears and block out his voice, anything not to hear what he was going to say.

"I'm sorry to have to ask." He took her hands. "Please just tell me."

"A-Adam has hair like me. Kind of brownish red but more wavy than curly. He isn't as big as you, but he's tall."

"Your cousin, was his name Tobias? Tell me what he looks

like."

"They're dead, Gideon. Why are you asking me this?" Chloe realized her cheeks were wet. Was it raining?

"Just tell me." He squeezed her hands, but she hardly felt it. Cold had seeped into her bones.

"Tobias was taller than Adam, but he was skinny with black hair and dark eyes. He had pox as a boy, and his cheeks were scarred from it." Her voice was flat and tight. She had just enough breath to get the words out.

"Shit." Gideon stared at her, his expression grim.

Chloe's fear mixed with anger, whirling around inside her like a twister. "What is it? Dammit, Gid, tell me. Now."

"I think I found Granny and the girls. But..." He stopped, and she wanted to shake him.

"What? What is it?" This time she could barely hear herself over the roaring in her ears.

He leaned in close and pressed his forehead to hers. His breath caressed her cheek. "I think your brother and cousin were the ones who took them."

The next few minutes were blurry as Chloe tried to absorb what he said. His words repeated over and over in her head, but she could not make sense of them. Why would Adam and Tobias take Granny and the girls? They were family, they were *kin*, and nothing in the world was more important than kin. He had to be wrong, very wrong. It didn't make any sense.

Memories washed through her so fast, she had to close her eyes to see them. Adam teaching her to fish. Playing in the field with both him and Tobias. Chasing after them through mud puddles. Adam kissing her goodbye when he left for war, wearing the jacket Granny had made for him.

Too much. It was too much.

She bit her lip hard until she tasted blood, but she couldn't make a sound. If she screamed as loud as she was inside, whoever was over at the campfire would hear her. It wasn't her brother and cousin though. It just couldn't be.

"Chloe, I'm sorry. I'm so sorry," he crooned softly in her ear as he stroked her back.

Somehow she'd ended up on his lap, and she couldn't think of a better place to be. He gave her the comfort she needed, craved, when her heart was breaking and the world around her rained down pain.

"Not them."

"I think it is, honey. It doesn't matter, though, because whoever they are, we found them." He pulled her chin up until she finally looked at him. "We found them."

"We found them?" she parroted.

"Hard to believe, but yes, we did. Through every possible mistake, problem and bad luck, we found them." He pushed her chin up until she looked at him. "Those girls' ribbons and your sheer stubbornness got us here."

She stared into his beautiful blue eyes and realized two things at once. If they had found her family, their journey together was likely over. And against her head's better judgment, she didn't want it to be over.

"Didn't you say you loved me?" she blurted, trying to fight the pain at the thought of not being with Gideon any longer.

"Yes, I do. We can talk about that later. Now I need to get back and take care of those men. There are three of them, so I need to be careful, really careful." He set her back on the log and cupped her cheek. "Sit here until I come back. If you hear gunfire, you damn well better not try to help me."

She kept her mouth shut, but she wanted to tell him not to

order her around. It didn't matter if Gideon had guns; three-to-one odds were not good. He could be easily killed if the other men had guns too. There was no way she'd sit by and let that happen.

"You're still bossy."

He took the rifle from his saddle, kissed her one last time, then disappeared back into the night, as silent as the darkness around him. She had wanted to tell him she loved him too but couldn't manage to make the words come out of her mouth. It would be too much like giving up who she was, and Chloe wasn't ready for that.

She watched until she couldn't see him any longer, then she waited five very long minutes before she decided to follow him. Oh, she knew he'd be madder than a wet hen that she didn't stay put, but could he blame her? The man had to know her well enough by now to remember she didn't listen to orders, especially from a man, even Gideon.

Chloe's gait was much less graceful than Gideon's, and she couldn't run at all. She turned to eye the horses and decided if she unsaddled the mare, she could make an almost silent approach. If there were no buckles to jangle, she could keep to the soft pine needles, and no one would hear her.

She knew how to shoot a gun, and she had one within reach. No way she'd led Gideon go off by himself to fight her battle. Not when she had a breath in her body. And if he yelled at her, she just might shoot him.

It took another five minutes before she got the saddle off and pulled herself up onto the mare's back. It had been a few years since she rode bareback, but as soon as she was upright, it came back to her in a flash. She threaded her fingers through the horse's mane and leaned down low to whisper, "C'mon, girl, we're going to see what my man is doing."

She saw the glow of the campfire in the distance and knew it wouldn't take long to get there.

Gideon followed his path back to the men who had taken what didn't belong to them. The veil of battle slipped over him and a calmness with it. Getting ready to fight was as familiar as breathing to him. Even years later, it was as comfortable as an old coat. Instead of struggling against it, he welcomed it.

The inky night surrounded him, giving him the cover he needed as he approached. The crackle of the fire was the only sound, and he wondered if the men were still there or if they were sleeping.

His breath came slow and steady, right along with his heartbeat. He crawled up behind the same tree and peered around. The two men, Tobias and Adam, were still sitting at the fire, but appeared to be dozing. Granny's eyes were also closed, which could either be good or bad. If she couldn't see him, she wouldn't give his presence away.

Every sound echoed in his ears as he crept closer. The rifle was warm in his hand, a comfortable presence. His grip tightened as he stood and stepped into the firelight, the rifle raised and braced against his shoulder. Only two of the men were visible, but he had to flush out the third.

"On your feet." His voice was loud in the silence.

Tobias jumped up as if someone had pinched him, his long arms flopping in panic. Adam, on the other hand, didn't do anything but push his hat back and stare hard at Gideon.

"I said on your feet."

"I don't take orders from nobody no more." Adam's eyes, similar to Chloe's, glittered like hard stones. He didn't appear to be as surprised as his cousin was, and that worried Gideon.

"Then I put a new hole to match that big one in the middle of your face." Gideon stepped sideways, careful to avoid rocks and sticks until he was positioned to shoot either of the men. "Now throw the guns behind you."

"I ain't throwing my gun," Tobias whined.

"It's *my* gun, and you are going to throw it, or it will be the last thing you hold in your hands." Gideon kept his voice even and hard. The sight of this bastard holding the gun he'd had for ten years made his blood boil. He couldn't even look at Granny, at how she'd been treated, or he would have shot the two men where they stood. There was still danger from the unseen man and the two pistols right in front of them.

If he shot them, Chloe would never forgive him.

"I know who you are." Adam sneered at him. "I saw you with Chloe like a randy buck sniffing a willing cunt."

Gideon's jaw nearly cracked from the pressure of grinding his teeth together. "You're the son of a bitch who kidnapped his own family."

The barb hit the mark, judging by the narrowing of the other man's eyes.

"This here is my property. I'm the oldest, and that bitch sister of mine stole it. I took it back and gave her what she deserved." Adam took a step closer, and Gideon dug his heels in, waiting for whatever the other man was going to do.

"Yeah, what she deserved." Tobias spoke up, emboldened by his cousin's cool demeanor. "Fucking nothing."

Gideon had no idea how these two were so twisted, so different from Chloe, who would sacrifice her life for family. The war had turned many men into different people, and obviously had done much worse to these Ruskin boys. Their souls had been blackened enough to blot out anything of their life prior to the conflict. It saddened him, but he had to push that thought aside and focus on what they were doing. Tobias took a step to the right, widening the gap between them.

"I'm giving you to the count of ten to drop the guns." A bead of sweat snaked down Gideon's back. He never took his gaze off the men threatening him. His heart thumped hard when he spotted movement under the wagon.

Chloe.

She never listened! She'd obviously made her way over to the camp and was trying to free her grandmother. Luckily for her, the men's backs were to the wagon, but that didn't account for the third man, an unknown and unseen enemy somewhere either in the wagon or nearby.

He wanted to shout at her to get back, but he dare not give her position away or let his attention wander for a second from the men with guns directly in front of him.

"Ten. Nine. Eight."

Granny disappeared from view under the wagon, and he was glad Chloe did not have to witness the gunfight with her kin. She still might never forgive him.

"He ain't really gonna shoot us, is he?" Tobias jigged in place as he looked at the rifle in Gideon's hand.

Gideon shot the ground beside Tobias, making the younger man yelp and jump a foot in the air.

"Yes, I really will shoot you. Seven. Six. Five."

The bead of sweat was joined by half a dozen more. His hand tightened on the pistol grip. He knew he could shoot one of them before they could get a shot off at him. The rifle in Adam's hand was the slower weapon, so he would shoot Tobias first.

"Four. Three."

"Adam, I don't want to die."

"You're a coward and no cousin of mine." Spittle flew from Adam's mouth as he bashed his cousin in the cheek with the rifle. Blood sprayed from the thin man's mouth, and he stumbled backward.

It was the opportunity Gideon needed. He launched himself at Adam with a split-second thought to Chloe that he loved her.

Chloe almost carried Granny out from under the wagon, which was difficult on any day, but with a sore knee, it was incredibly hard. Gideon was facing down her gun-toting brother and cousin, who were nearly unrecognizable now from the young men she'd known.

Grief threatened to overwhelm her, but she kept it locked away inside, refusing to allow it to escape. She still had to find the girls, and Gideon might need her.

Chloe set Granny down on a patch of grass in the shadow of the wagon. "Stay here, and I'll be back with the girls."

"Chloe, honey, I'm sorry." Granny never cried, but darned if tears were not sliding down her cheeks. "I thought they was here to help, and instead they did harm."

Chloe hugged Granny and whispered, "Love you, Granny."

She couldn't sit and talk, couldn't waste one moment while the man she loved was in danger. Chloe crept back as quietly and as quickly as she could, not stopping to wonder how she could help. She picked up the rifle as she crawled under the wagon in time to see the men fighting, and Chloe's heart stopped. They were a jumble of arms and legs. Grunts and the sound of flesh hitting flesh echoed in the dark night. She watched, helpless to do anything without running the risk of shooting Gideon.

A shadow appeared from the front of the wagon, and Chloe pointed the rifle at it. Whoever it was moved closer. The firelight reflected off a knife in his hand. Fury roared through her at the bastard who stalked the man she loved, the hero who was about to give his life for her family. Ignoring everything, including her pain, she rose to her feet, the rifle ready to fire.

Time slowed to a crawl as she got a bead on the shadowed stranger. A log crackled loudly, spraying sparks into the night air, giving her the light she needed to see the bastard.

The gun boomed in her hand, deafening in the darkness, silencing the night creatures. The big man crumpled to the ground, his knife falling into the dirt. The three men tussling stopped only momentarily before someone reached out and picked up the knife.

She couldn't get the rifle loaded fast enough to stop that blade from plunging into Gideon's shoulder. Chloe heard screaming and realized it was her own voice echoing into the night. She ran toward the men, ready to fight to the death to save Gideon.

The knife slid into his flesh before he could stop it. The pain radiated out like pure fire, intense and excruciating, but he had to ignore it. It wasn't the first time he'd been stabbed, and he had to shut the pain away or he would be dead. Chloe's brother was stronger than he looked, perhaps madness had lent him an extra dose of strength. Gideon couldn't even think about Chloe and the damn rifle blast. When she let loose a battle cry, he felt a surge of pride for her.

"Jesus, Chloe, what are you doing?" Tobias sounded shocked, and Gideon fought the insane urge to laugh. The man obviously had no idea what Chloe was capable of.

It was her family and her fight. Gideon wanted to shoot both men for hurting her, then leave them for the scavengers to feed on.

"Now both of you stop." Chloe stood there with both pistols in her grasp. Somehow she'd gotten hold of them. Her hands and her voice were like steel, hard and steady.

Adam stared up at her, his eyes cold. "What are you doing, you little slut?"

She snorted. "Names can't hurt me, Adam, but these bullets sure can hurt you."

To Gideon's amazement, she cocked both weapons. A shiver raced down his spine at the deadly fury in her expression.

"You ain't gonna shoot me, sissy." Adam rose to his feet, followed by Tobias, leaving Gideon to bleed alone on the ground.

This tiny scrap of a woman, who had more courage than most men, stood down her brother and cousin without flinching.

"Hell yes I will." She looked back and forth between them. "You stopped being my kin when you went rogue."

"Rogue?" Adam's laugh was chilling. "Girl, you ain't got no idea what I done if you think taking the wagon is bad." He moved closer to her, and Gideon got to his knees, trying to rise while pressing his hand into the knife wound.

"Shoot him, Chloe."

"I will, Gid. First I want to find out why." She let a bit of her hurt show in her eyes.

Adam, being a predator, recognized the pain beneath the anger. "Why? The world ain't no happy place no more, sissy. People kill each other for a fucking biscuit. You sold that damn farm out from under me, then packed up everything and headed to Texas." He was only three feet from her now, and Gideon couldn't stop him.

They were both going to die out here, and he was

powerless. He'd survived a lot, including a war and things that would have broken a lesser man, yet here he was, about to die for a woman. He wished he had married her and had beautiful babies with her before all was said and done. Now he wouldn't have the chance because of her crazy family.

"Why didn't you go home?" Gideon's voice was rough and full of pain. He cursed his own weakness.

"Ain't no home to go to, stupid." Adam focused on the pistols in Chloe's hands.

"After the war there was. It's been years, Ruskin. Why didn't you go home before now?" Gideon knew he'd found exactly what would shake the man's self-control when Adam's face flushed.

"I ain't got to tell you nothing. You fuck my sister and then question me? I will fuck your eye sockets before I cut you into pieces." A dark, twisted madness had stolen who Adam Ruskin had been and turned him into an unrecognizable monster. A monster who would steal children, beat an old woman and kill his own sister. He shook with rage as he looked between Gideon and Chloe. "Those girls are worth a fortune in Mexico. I was gonna take them before, but then this jackass came along and emptied the wagon for us. Made it easy for me to take what was mine."

"Mexico? You aren't going to make it a mile before we stop you." Gideon managed to stand and shake off the lightheaded feeling from blood loss. He couldn't fail her now, not when she needed him most. To prepare himself, he stood on the balls of his feet, ready to attack or defend.

"Your man here has a big mouth." Adam's hands fisted. "I'm gonna enjoy killing him."

"Adam, how could you do this?" Chloe's hands began to shake. "I loved you."

Adam shook his head. "Love died a long time ago, sissy. I take care of myself now and nobody else."

Gideon watched the other man's face and knew the exact moment the man chose his victim. Adam launched himself at Chloe, and Gideon's howl split the night air. He'd forgotten about Tobias though, distracted by the danger to his woman. Stars exploded in the back of his head, and the ground met his face with a painful slap.

Chapter Ten

Chloe jumped back before Adam could reach her. She didn't want to kill him, so she aimed for his foot and fired. He screeched and stumbled backward just as Gideon fell to the ground, Tobias standing behind him with a tree branch in his hand.

Now it was up to her and only her. They'd either killed or wounded Gideon, and Chloe had to think fast, or all of them might die.

When four shadows appeared and approached the fire, she knew a moment of despair. Six men against one were insurmountable odds. She'd die fighting though. While her brother cursed and tried to get to her, she stepped sideways toward Gideon, ready to defend him until she had no more life in her body.

"Don't go near him, lady." A blond man with the coldest brown eyes she'd ever seen walked toward her, guns drawn. Three more behind him had equally deadly weapons and the look of trained killers.

"I'll kill you if you touch him." She bared her teeth at him.

"Looks like Gid found himself a woman worthy of a devil." A one-armed man had Tobias on the ground, a foot on his back.

"I said get away from him." The cold-eyed blond came closer.

"She's not going to hurt him, Zeke." A brown-haired man with impeccably clean clothes had his gun trained on a screeching Adam. "She's defending him."

The one called Zeke glanced at the guns in her hands, then at Gideon. "That so?"

"That's so. Now get your men out of here before I kill all of you." She had never felt so scared or alive in her life. They were helping her, but they were still a threat.

"Ma'am, we're Gideon's friends, his family." The redheaded one held up his hands as he walked closer. "We came to help, but obviously he already had you." He smiled, and something inside Chloe gave way. She was ready for help and decided she had to trust them.

She fell to her knees and pulled Gideon's head into her lap. She managed not to vomit at the sight of the blood on his shirt, but it was damn hard. Oh God, her family had done this to him. She wanted to weep at the heavens and scream until she was raw, but she didn't.

"He's been stabbed and beaten. We need someone to doctor him." She kissed his cheek, so overwhelmed with emotion she barely recognized her own voice.

"Oh hell, she's gonna cry." The one-armed man sighed.

"Shut up, Lee. Let her do what she needs to." The redheaded one knelt beside her. "It's going to be okay. I can help him if you let me."

Chloe nodded and gave over care of her man to this stranger with the kind eyes. She stumbled toward the wagon to find the girls, to find her composure, before she cried and lost control completely.

The girls peered out from the wagon with identical expressions of relief when they saw her. As she gathered them into her arms, she let the tears fall.

Finally, finally, they'd found her family, for better or worse. They were safe.

Gideon heard voices but a haze had settled over his mind, and he had trouble focusing on them. For some reason, he heard Zeke and Nate, then Jake and Lee. He knew he was either dying or had been hit on the head so hard he was dreaming with vivid clarity.

"There's a sewing box under the wagon seat." Chloe sounded worried. Maybe she was in the dream too.

"He's breathing, but he's bleeding like a stuck pig." Lee never did mince words.

"That's not especially helpful information, Lee." Nate's voice was crisp as always. "Perhaps you can find something to help stanch the wounds."

A tearing sound preceded something being pressed into his shoulder. A roar of pain erupted from his mouth.

"He's awake. Where the hell is that girl with the sewing kit? We need to close up that wound on his shoulder." Zeke usually took charge when Gideon couldn't. He loved to give orders.

"I ran to the wagon on a bum leg, you ass," Chloe responded in her prickly way. "One of you could have gone to get it."

Soon there were many hands touching him. He opened his eyes and looked around, amazed to see everyone he loved and who was most important to him in the world.

His family. For some reason, Lee was bare-chested, and Gideon realized the item currently being used to mop up blood was Lee's shirt.

Chloe was handing implements to Jake, who was patiently sewing up the knife wound on his shoulder. The needle pricks were nothing compared to the agony left by the blade.

"Ouch," he managed to whisper.

She glanced at him, and the love he saw in her face hit him like a punch.

"I'm sorry." She shook her head, that crazy wild hair of hers swaying back and forth. "I'm sorry he stabbed you."

"He's been stabbed before." Jake grinned at him. "Survived it too. One more scar to show off to the ladies." He waggled his brows.

"Lady. Just one lady." He glanced at Chloe again, but she looked away.

"Ah, so it's true. You found somebody." Jake was always the teaser, the foolish one who lightened the darkest moments. "And she's meaner than Zeke."

"You know it would help if you stopped making jokes, Red." Lee leaned over and touched Gideon's head. "It would help if you didn't die either, Gid."

His eyes pricked with unwanted tears as he took in how much his family was worried about him. No matter what happened, or how bad things got, he always had them.

"He ain't gonna die, so shut up." Zeke must've tied up Tobias and Adam. They sat on the ground, tied up like prizes for the nearest sheriff.

"How are you here?" Gideon managed to ask.

"You sent a wire to me, remember? Scared everyone to death saying you'd been robbed and were helping some family." Zeke scowled. "We rode to Westville right away to do what we could. After some convincing, they told us which way you'd headed."

"The German man in the stables was a little tight-lipped until we told him who we were." Lee's expression matched his brother's. "You made an impression on that town."

"Nice folks there." Gideon remembered how Daisy had helped Chloe with new clothes, and how beautiful she'd looked. His heart pinched at the memory.

"The sheriff made us wait while he sent a wire to verify who Zeke was. Those folks liked you, but they sure as hell didn't like us." Jake shook his head.

The people of Westville didn't trust a group of four armed, large men riding into town? How shocking. Gideon didn't bother pointing out just how intimidating they were.

"You tracked us." It wasn't a question. Gideon knew the answer.

"Yep, we did. Lee is still the best." Zeke's fierce expression softened. "You really had us worried."

"Sorry. Had to do what I had to do."

The four of them had no need to respond. They understood what he meant and likely would have done the same thing, especially for a woman they loved.

"Chloe." Gideon wanted to grab her hand, but he couldn't quite make his arms move yet.

"I'm busy, let me be." She still did not look at him.

"What's wrong?"

"Nothing's wrong. Shut up and let me work."

"Should I leave?" Jake looked between them.

"No, I won't shut up." Gideon dug deep inside and found the strength to get to one elbow and grab her chin. Much as she fought it, he finally made her look at him. "I love you, Chloe Ruskin. You're a maddening, bossy little slip of a woman, but there you have it. I love you."

She stared at him as his heart thumped madly. Jake tried to keep sewing up the wound, while blood slid in a warm stream down Gideon's arm.

"I...I can't." She yanked her chin out of his grasp, and he swore she dashed away some tears.

"Coward." He was putting himself and his heart at risk one last time. If she didn't give him what he needed to keep living, hell, keep breathing, then he'd somehow manage to let her go.

"I ain't a coward, Blackwood." She slammed the torn strip of cloth into Jake's hand.

"You'd better do something, Gid, before she hurts both of us," Jake said under his breath.

"I heard that." Chloe glared at his redheaded half brother. "I ain't deaf and stupid, you know."

Gideon knew she was sliding away from him, emotionally and mentally. She was closing up on herself, and he'd watched it happen. He had spent a lifetime looking for her, and he'd be damned if he let her pride get in the way.

"Chloe Ruskin, will you marry me?"

Her mouth dropped open, and she wasn't alone. All the Devils stared at him slack-jawed.

"Holy shit."

"Did he just ask her to marry him?"

"Maybe it's the blood loss."

"Maybe it's love." Jake looked between them, and his grin grew as wide as the sky. "I think, fellow Devils, that we have ourselves a genuine case of true love."

Chloe shook her head and started to back away. Gideon wasn't about to let that happen. He grabbed her uninjured leg and crawled toward her, the bloody needle and thread dangling from his arm. A whoosh echoed through his head and the world tilted a bit, but he ignored it. All that mattered was Chloe.

"That blood's not very romantic."

"Didn't you propose in a barn?"

"I think it was a jail cell."

"Shut up, all of you." Zeke hushed them up.

All Gideon saw was Chloe. All he heard was her heart beating in concert with his. He managed to press up against her and kiss her parted lips.

"Marry me. I love you, Chloe." His voice broke on her name, his heart unable to contemplate life without the little curmudgeon who had taken up permanent residence in its chambers.

"I-I love you too." She stuttered on each syllable. "B-but my kin tried to k-kill you." She shook so hard her bones rattled together.

Chloe Ruskin was scared.

"Ah, honey, my kin is a bunch of crazy ex-soldiers who have drinking problems, missing limbs and surly dispositions. You can't pick your family, but you can pick your wife." He pressed his forehead to hers. "Please, Chloe, say yes."

Her breath puffed out in gasps as he held his until he thought he'd pass out from lack of air.

"Yes." Her whisper was barely audible, but he heard it.

Gideon closed his eyes to keep away the tears that threatened at the joy he felt in that one little word. It marched through his body, leaving him trembling as much as she was.

The last Devil had finally found where he belonged. In Chloe Ruskin's arms.

Over the course of two days, they rode slowly back to Westville as a group, Gideon in the wagon with Granny and the girls. Adam and Tobias walked behind them, tied at the wrist and to Zeke's saddle. At night she hardly slept a wink, watching

Gideon to make sure he didn't die. Their journey was a relatively quiet one, except for Adam and Tobias complaining.

Chloe drove the team and listened for Gideon, making sure he didn't sound as though he was in too much pain. She didn't want him to fall out of the wagon if he passed out again. When she'd suggested it might happen, he looked at her as if she had grown a second head.

She might have laughed, but she was afraid he would be more offended. She wisely held in the unwanted mirth, swallowing it down amidst the emotions churning in her gut. She swung between joy, disbelief and misery. How could the most amazing thing in her life coincide with the absolute worst? Her brother was a monster, and his blood ran through her veins. What did that say about her?

How could Gideon ignore that? His family consisted of honorable men, albeit rough around the edges. The fact her family was a river of dirt should send him running the other direction. Yet he didn't. In fact, the foolish man had proposed to her. It had nearly sent her running. He'd been sincere, and she'd seen the love in his eyes, heard it in his voice. Chloe should have said no, should have ignored the tug she felt in her heart every time she saw him.

But she couldn't and she hadn't. Chloe had said yes to his proposal, and now panic raced through her as the reality of marrying Gideon slammed into her. He came from a high-society family, was a good man who deserved more than the ignorant daughter of a dirt farmer with thieving murderers for kin.

Some of his family were noisy and talkative, while others were quiet. The four men were as big as Gideon, and together they were more intimidating than anything she'd experienced, which was saying a lot. She could imagine how formidable they had been during the war. They still were. Chloe liked the redheaded man, Jake. He smiled a lot, putting her at ease, as much as she could be at ease. He was also funny, earning sharp comments from the blond men, Zeke and Lee. The dark-haired, well-dressed man, Nate, was unfailingly polite and used words she didn't understand.

This was the family she would be marrying into, and they not only scared her, they made her wonder if she should disappear once they arrived in Westville. As much as she fought against it, her love for Gideon had become firmly entrenched in her heart, in her soul. There would be no other man in her life to take his place, no matter what happened.

With her stomach in a knot, the big group rode through Westville, earning a few curious stares from the late-night inhabitants, which made her want to laugh like a crazy woman. The nice folks in this little town had no idea what they were getting into when they had helped Gideon and Chloe a few days earlier. Now the Blackwood clan had descended on them.

"Where to?"

"The doctor's place is down the street a bit. He took care of Chloe after the horse fell on her leg." Gideon looked pale and sweaty, and his bloody shirt made her want to turn away and hide. She didn't even want to consider what would happen if he died. She'd already accepted him into her life; to lose him now would devastate her.

"A horse fell on her leg?" Jake looked her over, as if assessing just how clumsy she was. "How did that happen?"

"An accident," was her only response. She didn't want to talk to them about it. It still saddened her to think of the horse's death. The trauma of that moment would live in her memories for years. No need to relive it so soon after it happened.

"I think we need to sit down and hear the entire story." Zeke eyed them both with an intense stare. "Naomi almost kicked me out the door to come help you. The wire you sent turned Tanger on its ear."

Chloe assumed Naomi was his wife, and she tried to imagine what Gideon had put in his wire that affected an entire town.

"After the doctor looks at him." She wasn't about to let them risk his life to hear the entire almost unbelievable story.

Zeke raised one brow and turned to look at Gideon. "She's a smaller version of you, Captain."

Three of the men chuckled. Gideon narrowed his eyes at them.

"Shut up, all of you. Now is not the time to make jokes." When he looked at Chloe, she saw the pain lines in his face and the exhaustion in his eyes. However, his voice had been hard and sharp, one she'd heard before, but this time it made all the men obey. He did have a captain's tone, and he obviously still commanded his men. "Zeke, you and Lee take these two over to the sheriff's office. Jake and Nate, come with me to the doctor."

Chloe wondered for a moment if married life would be a series of orders she would endure. Then Gideon surprised her once more.

"Chloe, honey, will you come with us to the doctor?" Gone was the commanding man, and in his place a soft lover.

She melted like hot grease on a skillet inside, but outside she merely shrugged. "I reckon I don't have anything else to do right now."

"I like her. She certainly has the captain tamed." Jake winked at her, and Chloe had to look away, or she'd embarrass herself by smiling at the charming man.

These people would break down her defenses before she knew it. She couldn't let that happen too easily. Granny and the girls were her first responsibility.

Granny was surprisingly quiet, sitting with the sleeping girls on either side of her in the back of the wagon. Chloe's heart ached for them, for what they had endured at the hands of Adam and Tobias. She needed to talk to her, but Gideon's safety came first. The wide-eyed girls had been well-behaved, and Chloe grew even more worried. Once he was safe, she would take care of finding out what had happened to them. None of them appeared to be injured, aside from wrists rubbed raw from ropes.

When they arrived at the doctor's house, Granny waved Chloe away, apparently content to wait in the wagon. She had obviously heard everything that went on with Gideon but still said nothing. The entire business with the man had Granny's approval from the start, and now that he'd proposed, she was quiet as a mouse.

Something was definitely wrong.

The doctor was no less grumpy than he had been the first time they visited him, but she didn't have to endure his doctoring either. It was the middle of the night, and he was not at all pleased to have a patient. Gideon's bloody appearance made him admit them immediately. This time she sat in the parlor while Gideon's friends carried him into the examining room. She should have gone in with him, but the truth was she needed a chance to think. The idea of being in the examining room again made her skin crawl. Chloe did not like doctors, especially this one.

Unfortunately, she didn't get the chance to be alone. Jake and Nate appeared in the parlor after she sat down. The redhead still had bloodstains on his shirt from stitching up

Gideon, and she could barely look at him. It was Gideon's blood, spilled by her brother.

Her stomach flipped upside down again.

"Don't run. I promise we'll behave." Jake sat on the edge of the dusty settee while Nate stood near the doorway, looking just as neat as he had before.

"I will behave in any case, Chloe."

"Fine." She wanted to go check on her family but also wanted to simply be still for a few minutes.

"Chloe, I know it's been a rough week for you. Gideon actually warned us not to bother you." Jake had a beautiful smile. "But we're worried about you too. Are you okay?"

She forced herself to smile. "I won't be until I know he is."

Jake laughed. "Now she sounds like Zeke. A woman of few words." He winked at her again, and she looked away. They were talking to her as if they knew her, as if she were already part of their family. A lump blossomed in her throat.

"Stop teasing her. Let her take a few moments to gather her thoughts." Nate appeared formal on the outside, but she saw concern in his eyes, and she was grateful for it. "She's been hurt too."

Her concern for Gideon became an ache in her chest, intense enough that she barely remembered the pain in her leg. She couldn't just sit there and do nothing. Maybe Granny needed her. She got to her feet, ready to escape, when both of the men rose too.

"Where are you going?" Jake's tone wasn't accusatory, but it was definitely not a casual question either.

"I need to get out of here. My feet are itching to move." She was jumpy, unsure of herself and about to run like a scared rabbit.

Jake took her hand, his cool and calloused. "Please don't run away because of us. We are worried about Gid, and we tend to be a little, ah, overwhelming when that happens." He gestured to the settee. "Please, sit down before Gid has our heads for chasing you off."

She contemplated leaving the building, but then she wouldn't know how Gideon was doing, and that might just drive her completely loco.

"No more questions?"

Both of them nodded. She was grateful for the reprieve. This time when she sat down, they moved to the opposite corner of the room, talking quietly. She managed to sit still and maintain her dignity while her mind whirled in circles. One horrible thought was followed by another. After ten minutes, the silence was bothering her. She knew she appeared fickle to the two men, but Chloe needed to talk.

"You know, when the wheel broke on our wagon, I never thought I'd meet someone like Gideon. No one wanted to help us until he came along." She remembered clearly the moment she first saw him, how her entire body leapt to life at the sight of the broad-shouldered man on the horse. He caught her eye from that very second. Strange how life brought them together, and how many obstacles had been thrown in their path after that first meeting. "Then he was there to help me when somebody took the girls."

"He's got more honor than anyone I know." Nate's voice was full of pride.

"Me too." Chloe almost choked on the half sob, half laugh that exploded from within her. She felt so blessed to have found him, to love him, yet so scared of what it all meant.

"No matter what happens, we're here for you and Gideon. Think of us as your family now." Jake's smile had been tucked away. "Do you want us to go with you to talk to the sheriff?"

She had a feeling they wanted to talk about Adam and Tobias, but she had no answers for them. "No, I ain't ready for that yet."

"I can understand your reluctance." Nate touched her hand. "Let us know when you are."

Chloe's throat closed up at the way they'd simply accepted her. These were good folks, better than her own family.

"He wants to see you." The doctor appeared in the doorway, waving his hand impatiently. "He's a worse patient than you, if that's at all possible."

Chloe got to her feet and managed not to run out of the building although she wanted to. There was no need to be afraid, yet she was. He'd asked her to marry him, but that didn't mean he wouldn't change his mind or worse.

"Down the hall on the left." The doctor disappeared into the back of the house.

The walk down the hall seemed longer than it should, as her mind turned over all the possibilities of what could happen. The door was slightly ajar, a glow coming through the crack. Her hand shook as she pushed it open far enough to slip in.

Gideon lay on the cot, surrounded by white sheets and bandages. He looked incredibly pale as though he'd lost some of his life along with the blood. It spooked her badly to see him like that. He'd been strong every moment she'd been with him, and now he was weak and wounded.

His eyes were closed, his lashes dark smudges on his cheeks. She studied him for a moment, wondering how God thought to put this man in her path, to collide with him, truth be told. They clashed, fought, argued, and still managed to fall in love.

Love.

Gideon had told her days before that he loved her. She'd struggled against it, not able to tell him how she felt. Then, when he'd been bloodied and perhaps dying, she'd finally admitted her love to him. It had been liberating and at the same time, terrifying. Words she couldn't take back, another bell she couldn't unring. For better or worse, she had confessed her deepest secret, and a lightning bolt didn't strike her down, his love had.

"You about done ogling me?" His voice was rough and rusty, not his usual deep tone.

She somehow didn't blush at his question; instead she ignored it and perched on the side of the bed. He took her hand, which was warm and so alive. A rush of emotion washed over her, and her eyes pricked with tears.

"Don't cry for me, honey. I'll live."

She couldn't explain what made those damn tears appear, and she wished they'd go back where they came from. However, if wishes were horses, beggars would ride, and she was still on foot. Chloe shook her head and pushed back against the emotions swirling through her.

"I ain't crying for you."

"Good to know. I wouldn't want to be the one who made you cry." He squeezed her hand.

"You're not, so don't worry." His humor allowed her self-control to take over again. "You in pain?"

He tried to shrug but managed only to wince. "Some."

"Doc give you something for the pain or do I need to?" She remembered too vividly how it felt to be in pain and have the laudanum in her system. Gideon deserved a dose of that himself.

"Yes he did, no need to take revenge." He knew her too well already.

She stared into his blue eyes, lost in the depths. "You make me crazy."

"You make me want to get drunk."

"You boss me around too much."

"You argue too much."

This time when she laughed, he smiled at her, and the beauty of it made her breath catch. "I love you, Chloe Ruskin."

She had held back much of herself, had spent so long worrying about her family, and his softly spoken words broke the dam within her.

"I love you too, Gideon Blackwood."

Chloe finally let the walls fall away and gave her heart and soul to Gideon Blackwood. As she laid her head beside his on the cot and let his warmth seep into hers, she knew she'd found where she belonged.

Gideon woke to the sound of someone clearing his throat. He cracked his eyes open to find all four of the Devils standing over him. If he was a lesser man, he might have been afraid, but he knew they were just checking on him.

"I'm still alive, so go back to Tanger."

Zeke scowled deeply. "Not funny, Captain. We came to help you, and we're not leaving. I will travel home with you by my side or not at all."

"My sentiments exactly." Nate crossed his arms and joined in the staring.

"He needs to stay in Tanger." Lee sat on the only chair in the room, his back against the wall.

"I'd be happy if he did." Jake grinned at him. "Now that he's found himself a woman, I think we can count on it."

Gideon was glad of their loyalty, but sometimes it was too much. "You ought to be nicer to me. I'm wounded."

They all laughed, finding humor in his feeble excuse. He'd definitely been wounded much worse and gotten up on both feet to fight before a bandage ever touched him too. The thought of being taken care of by Chloe while he healed, however, made him almost glad he'd been wounded.

"I'll stay in Westville until Chloe is ready to leave." Gideon pushed up into a sitting position slowly, glad the room didn't spin anymore. The laudanum must have worn off. "Zeke, what happened to Adam and Tobias?"

"They're in the jail. The sheriff wired the district judge. He'll be here in a couple of days to decide whether or not to hold them over for trial." Zeke shook his head. "Shame that two good Southern boys turned rotten."

"What about Chloe? How is she doing?"

"She's fine. We made her lie down in the parlor. She's in there snoring now, so we snuck in to see you. That little woman is a fierce guard dog." Jake patted his leg. "When you're ready, we'll take you over to the hotel and get out of this doctor's cave. He isn't the nicest sort, is he?"

"No, but he patched Gid up." Lee got to his feet. "He would've had some trouble if he hadn't."

Gideon stared at them one by one, noting the furtive glances between them and what they weren't saying. "Why are the four of you really here?"

"We've never seen you act like you do with her." Zeke jerked his thumb toward the door. "Can she be trusted?"

Gideon swallowed the bark of annoyance that threatened to

pop out of his mouth. Zeke was only concerned about Gideon, not talking badly about Chloe. After all, Zeke didn't know her or anything about her other than her brother and cousin were potential murderers.

"Yes, with my life."

"Good enough for me," Jake piped up. "Besides, I like her."

The rest of them murmured their assent. The knot in Gideon's stomach loosened. "I'm going to marry her."

"We heard." Nate smiled. "Unusual place for a proposal. The bloody needle dangling from your shoulder will live in infamy."

Gideon laughed. "At least she said yes." He grinned, letting the memory of her softly worded *I love you too* float through his memory.

"About time too. We were getting tired of the bachelor in the family." Lee punched his good shoulder lightly. "I thought I'd be the last one to get hitched."

"I'm glad for you, cousin. Really glad." Zeke squeezed his arm.

"Wait until the women hear about this." Jake chuckled. "Your wedding will be a regular town event. You bringing her grandmother and the two little girls with you?"

"I want to, but I haven't talked to Chloe yet." He thought about what the three of them had been through and wondered just how much damage the Ruskin boys had done. As soon as he could, he'd find time to talk to Granny.

"A family." Nate smiled and shook his head. "Another family to take care of."

"Ah, but this is different." Gideon pointed at his friend. "These ladies aren't lazy good-for-nothings who whine all the time."

That started a tussle between the two of them, and within minutes they were all laughing and smiling like crazy men. Gideon looked around at his family and knew they had all finally conquered the damage done to them during the war. He was whole again.

Chloe walked to the jail with Nate on one side and Jake on the other. True to their word, they escorted her to talk to her family, and their protectiveness gave her some measure of strength to do what she had to do.

When she stepped into the jail, her entire body shook with anger and fear. The sheriff sat behind the desk. He nodded at them but didn't speak. Adam and Tobias got to their feet as soon as they spotted her. More than the bars of the cell separated them though.

"'Bout time you showed up, Chloe. We need to get out of here. You need to see to it," Adam snapped. "And who the hell are they?"

She glanced at Nate. "Can you two wait outside while I talk to them?"

He scowled. "Gideon wouldn't like it."

"I'm not Gideon."

"She's got you there." Jake squeezed her shoulder. "Just give a shout if you need us." He pulled Nate out the door, leaving Chloe standing by herself.

Her feet felt nailed to the floor. It was harder to face them now than it had been by the light of the fire days earlier.

"Well? What are you gonna do about getting us out of here?" Adam's sharp words got her moving again.

She stepped toward them, her throat dry and heart smacking against her ribs. "I want some answers."

Adam snorted. "I don't care what you want, little sister. I want to get out of here."

"Me too." Tobias had lost all his bravado once he was behind bars. He looked like the boy she remembered too well, wide-eyed and scared.

"Where were you?" The anger began to push away the fear. "We needed you at home, and you never came back."

Adam snorted. "I didn't want to come back. There was nothing to come back to. A dirt farm, a pain-in-the-ass sister and an old woman? Nothing."

His words cut like broken glass. "We're family. We're not nothing."

This time he bared his teeth. "I learned how to make quick money, how to take care of *me*. Ain't nobody else matters but me."

"Then I feel sorry for you. Nothing matters but family." Grief for who he had been and for what he'd become filled her heart.

"Do you know I killed a man for his shoes? It was war, Chloe, and my feet were bleeding. Does that make me a murderer or a survivor?" Adam's voice started to rise, sounding fractured and frantic. "I did what I had to."

"No, you had a choice, Adam. I loved you. You're my brother, and you always had a home to come back to." She wrapped her arms around herself and shivered at the emotions in the air.

"I had no choice. I did too much, saw too much. I wasn't going to be the same fool I was when I left home." His eyes were full of darkness and shadows. Adam was not her brother any longer—he had become a monster.

"Then I feel sorry for you." Her heart knew it was time to

say goodbye to them.

"Fuck your pity."

She turned to her cousin, who had begun to weep silently. His large eyes were empty and hollow. "Goodbye, Tobias."

She turned to leave when Adam let loose a string of curses that crawled across her skin. War had truly turned them into ghosts of who they had been. She would grieve for them, no matter what the law decided to do with them.

"Goodbye, Adam." Chloe held the tears back until the door closed behind her. Nate and Jake never said a word as they handed her their handkerchiefs and waited while she wept in the dirt outside the jail in Westville.

Chloe had finally let go of her past.

Chapter Eleven

Three days later, Gideon was ready to get back to Tanger. Chloe argued with Lee all the time, while Granny argued with Zeke. The girls were running around like wild children, and Nate had taken to hiding with Jake somewhere in town.

Chloe hadn't left Gideon's side much, taking care of him. He appreciated her care, but it left him little time to talk to Granny. There was something bothering the older woman, and he wanted to find out what it was without hurting Chloe. She'd already been hurt enough.

That day, they had to face her brother and cousin again. He understood her pain, frustration and confusion at what they'd done. The traveling circuit judge had arrived in Westville, and it was time to hear what he planned on doing with the wayward Ruskins.

As Gideon dressed, his muscles protested, as did his healing wounds. With a few hisses and even more curses, he managed to pull on his trousers. By then he was sweating and regretting the fact he'd even tried. That's when Chloe walked in.

One brow went up. "What are you doing?"

"Trying to get my damn clothes on."

"Where do you think you're going?" She tapped one foot and folded her arms.

"To the judge with you."

Her mouth formed an O of surprise, and her arms fell away. "Really?"

His heart hurt for her at the idea she wouldn't expect him to be there when she needed him. "Of course I am. We're to be married. I'll always be by your side."

She looked at the floor and managed a small nod. "Thank you." Her voice was barely a whisper.

"You're welcome. Now help me get dressed before I fall down and make a mess." He was loath to admit he needed help, but at least it was Chloe and not one of the Devils. They'd never let him forget it.

With her assistance, he was dressed in a few minutes, and they made their way slowly out of the hotel. The judge was waiting at the jail for them, a tall, balding man, and whipcord lean. He nodded at them.

"Miss Ruskin. Mr. Blackwood. I'm Judge Henry. Nice to meet you."

They shook hands and stepped into the small jail. Gideon nodded at the sheriff. They'd met days earlier, which seemed like a lifetime ago. Chloe's hand danced within Gideon's like a trapped butterfly. She appeared as calm and tough as any man in the room, yet she showed him just how scared she was. He squeezed her hand, relieved to feel her return the gesture.

In the back of the building, the two Ruskin men sat in the jail cell, their arms dangling through the bars. They both looked hard at Chloe.

She looked as if she was going to say something but turned away from them and looked at the judge instead.

Nate stood by, the attorney of the Devils, ready to assist. "Judge Henry, I would not suggest there be any delay in transferring these men to Houston for trial."

"Let me do my job, Marchand." The judge's tone wasn't harsh, but he obviously didn't want any advice from Nate. He turned to Gideon. "I spoke to Miss Ruskin and her grandmother earlier about what transpired between you and these two men. I need to hear your tale too, before I make any decisions."

Chloe, surprisingly, kept silent. He wondered what she'd gone through when the judge talked to her. She hadn't said a word and certainly hadn't asked him to be there with her. Gideon had never met a stronger woman.

He told his story to the judge quickly, although he was sweating from the memory of believing Chloe and he had been about to die. A chair was shoved under him, and he sat down heavily. Someone handed him a handkerchief, and he wiped his face.

Judge Ruskin studied him for a few moments. "I believe there is sufficient evidence to hold Adam and Tobias Ruskin over for trial in Houston. I'll wire for an escort. Thank you both for your time." The judge murmured something to the sheriff, then left the jail.

Chloe stared at the floor while Gideon stared at her. She had a hand in making sure her family paid for their crimes. He wanted to get her alone so he could find out how she was feeling about that. It had to have been one of the hardest things she'd ever done.

"You bitch," Adam spat. "You steal my fucking property and that idiot judge has the nerve to send me to jail?"

Chloe looked at Gideon. "Let's get out of here before I say something stupid."

Gideon nodded his thanks to Nate, then rose, taking his woman's hand. As they walked out of the building together, Adam continued to scream at them. To her credit, she flinched only once.

The morning sunshine greeted them as if nothing had happened in the jail. Chloe took a deep breath and blew it out slowly. She squinted up at the sun. "I reckon we need to talk about things."

Gideon tucked her hand in the crook of his arm and started walking back toward the hotel. "What do you want to talk about?" He'd let her discuss whatever she wanted to.

Chloe had been through hell and back the last week. She deserved his ear, his hand, his heart. She deserved anything and everything he could give her.

"You, uh, asked me to marry you."

"I did."

"Did you mean it?"

Her soft question made his heart pinch. There was a plethora of hope and fear in those four little words, and they hit him square between the eyes.

"The only thing I meant more was telling you I love you." He patted her hand. "I still love you, and yes, I definitely want to marry you." Saying it out loud again made him smile. How could his life have changed so drastically in such a short period of time?

She let out a nervous laugh. "I just wanted to be sure. I mean, I don't come from very good stock. And my brother did try to kill you."

He stopped and turned to face her. "I don't blame you for anything Adam or Tobias did. Don't ever think for a moment I would. The war turned lots of men into dark creatures, and there's nothing you can do to change them back."

She stared up at him for a beat before she nodded. "I have to ask. I ain't gonna marry a man who doesn't know every terrible thing about me."

"Do I know every terrible thing?" He smiled down at her.

She nodded. "Yep. There's nothing left to tell."

With a whoop, he swung her around until she begged him to stop. Then he kissed her in front of the entire town of Westville.

"Will you make Tanger your home with me? I think that town was made for you." He would go wherever she needed to, but he wanted to stay in Tanger.

"If'n you want to live there, I'll live there. Martha and Hazel and Granny are included. It's a package of all four of us." Her voice had grown stronger, even a bit demanding.

"Hm, four for the price of one? I can't complain about that."

She swatted his arm. "You stop fooling with me now, Gideon Blackwood."

"I'm not fooling." He pulled her close until they were nose to nose. "I would love for all of you to come live with me in Tanger. We'll build a house and make babies and have a good life together."

Her eyes grew bright, and then she smiled shakily. "Let's go to Tanger."

It took another two days to repair the damage to the wagon, or rather, that was what they told Chloe. As she walked out of the hotel with Gideon, she stopped dead in her tracks. The wagon had been loaded with all their things. Her voice deserted her.

Tears sparkled in Granny's eyes as she stared at the belongings she'd thought she'd lost. Chloe's throat grew tight as she put her arm around her grandmother's small shoulders. When had she become frail and old? Granny was always the strong one in the family, the rock that Chloe clung to through all the storms.

"Look what those men did for us." Granny's voice shook. "I cain't believe they did that."

"They're good folks, Granny." Chloe kissed Granny's temple. "I haven't talked with you yet, but Gideon asked me to marry him."

Granny turned her head to look at her. "And I hope you said yes, girlie."

"Not the first time, but I did the second." Chloe grinned. "He wants us all to live with him in Tanger. I know we were on our way to see your sister…"

Granny shook her head. "Julia died last year. I didn't tell you because I wanted to leave Virginia, and I knew you wouldn't go unless there was a good reason." She swiped at her eyes. "You and those girls, you're all I have now. I thought Adam and Tobias—" Her voice broke, and Chloe pulled her into a hug. Granny made a small squeak as if she was in pain, and it echoed through Chloe's bones.

As they shared the deep, dark grief together, she saw Gideon watching them. His blue eyes reflected concern, but he didn't approach them, and for that Chloe was grateful. He seemed to know what she was thinking and feeling before she even did. If that was what love did to folks, then she was all for it.

"We have Gideon now too, and his family." Chloe closed her eyes and reined in her emotions. Hearing Granny's heartbreak over the Ruskin men was almost too much. She had just come to terms with what her kin had done, and knowing they were on their way to Houston to stand trial made the emotions wash over her again. Life definitely liked to throw in the good with the bad.

By the time she was able to let Granny go, Chloe was ready to let the past go as well. It would be a few days until they reached Tanger. The sooner they got started, the sooner they'd arrive at their new home.

"Ready?" Gideon stepped up beside them.

"Ready." Chloe had to stifle a giggle when she spotted Hazel and Martha running in circles around the stoic-faced Zeke. Arms folded, he watched them like a papa hawk.

"Let's get everybody loaded, then." Gideon turned to Zeke. "Stop playing with the twins, Zeke. Girls, come on, let's go."

Like his voice was magic, the two moppets stopped what they were doing and raced toward him. Yes, Chloe had definitely chosen the right man.

"All the ladies are waiting for you in Tanger." Gideon held out his hand for her. "I can hardly wait to see what they've planned."

She didn't know why the ladies were waiting for her, but she was excited to get to Tanger and find the place she could call home.

Within a few minutes, they were ready to go. When the group left Westville, Chloe was amazed at just how formidable the men were. Although Gideon rode in the wagon with Granny and the girls, his horse hitched to the back, the other four men rode tall in the saddle. They surrounded the wagon like a wall of men and guns.

Chloe had never felt so safe or so happy.

Chloe slept in the wagon, the girls squeezed between her and Gideon. Granny had insisted on bunking beneath the wagon. The rest of the men bedded down around them, keeping watch over them. Chloe had fallen asleep easily.

A noise startled her awake. She sat up and peered through the murky darkness at Hazel and Martha, but they were both asleep. Gideon was snoring lightly, but she didn't think that was what woke her. She stopped, still as the night around her, just as Gideon had taught her. Chloe strained to hear whatever had woken her.

A noise sounded again from outside the wagon, perhaps a wounded animal. Chloe crept out from her cocoon, pistol in hand, and landed barefoot on the cool, dew-covered ground. She stood still for a few moments, listening, then heard it again. It was coming from *under* the wagon.

Chloe dropped to her knees and crawled around the sleeping men to reach Granny. The older woman was barely a lump beneath the blankets and quilts around her.

"Granny?" Chloe touched her shoulder. "You okay?"

She thought she heard a response. Chloe lay on her side and scooted closer to her grandmother. "Granny?"

"Child." Her grandmother's voice was a broken whisper full of pain. "I thought I could make it to your man's town, but I cain't."

Panic clawed at Chloe as she struggled to focus on what was happening. "What are you talking about? Are you sick?"

"Not sick." Granny grabbed her hand. "That big bastard with Adam and Tobias kicked me in the belly when they wasn't looking. I think he broke me inside."

Chloe couldn't breathe for a moment. "What are you saying?" She moved closer until she was nearly nose to nose with her.

Granny's soft breath blew across her cheek. "I'm dying, child."

"No, you're not. Let me get Jake. He's good at doctoring. We can go back to Westville." Chloe managed to maneuver herself into a half-crouch to pull her grandmother out when she stopped. A terrible truth slapped her in the face. "You already saw the doctor in Westville, didn't you?"

Her grandmother had always been the strong one who led the family through thick and thin. Now she lay beneath a wagon dying, and there wasn't a damn thing Chloe could do to help her.

"Yep, fool man. He told me what I already knowed. I'm broke up inside and that's that." She pulled at Chloe's hand. "Now you listen. You got a good life coming your way. Don't let that pride of yours get in the way."

"Granny, I don't want to talk about me—"

"That's too damn bad." The older woman didn't give an inch. "You're going to talk about it with me."

"Please, let me get help." Chloe begged to help her, to do anything but sit there under the wagon in the dark and talk.

"I don't need no help. I'm dying and ain't nothing gonna change that." Granny squeezed her hands. "Promise me you're gonna snatch that chance for a good life and hang on to it."

"I can't." Tears ran freely down Chloe's cheeks as grief spilled from her heart.

"Yes, you can. Promise me." Her grip tightened until Chloe's bones rubbed together. Granny was still strong.

"I promise." The words were torn from her throat. "Now please, I can't just let you lie there and die." Chloe placed her hand on Granny's forehead and found more heat than should be there. Dread filled her as she realized Granny was slipping away. "Didn't the doctor give you medicine?"

"Bah, he gave me laudanum, but that ain't gonna cure me. It'll only make me sleep."

"It will stop the pain." Chloe lay back down and pressed her forehead to her granny's. "Oh God, don't leave me, please."

"Hush now, child. I'm old and had my life. It's your turn now. You've got a good man, two little girls to raise and a new family." Granny's voice was growing softer with each word. "Most of all, you got love."

As she'd done as a child, Chloe laid her head on her grandmother's chest and listened to the beat of her heart. It had always been a comforting place to be, where she felt most safe and loved. Now there were mere minutes, seconds, left to spend with her. A bucket of memories squeezed into a drop she couldn't hold on to. It was slipping through her fingers with every passing moment.

Thump. Thump. Thump.

Silence.

Granny slipped away without a sound. The end of a life so full, so amazing. Soul-wrenching pain roared through Chloe at the thought of facing the rest of her life without the woman who had shaped it. She opened her mouth and let loose a howl of pain so powerful it made the wagon boards above her shake.

Gideon woke to the sound of an animal screaming in anguish. He was on his feet outside the wagon in seconds, shirtless, barefoot but with his gun drawn. The other four Devils were also armed and awake. They all looked at each other and waited for the sound to repeat. The scream came again, and Gideon recognized the voice immediately.

"Chloe!" He dropped to his knees and crawled beneath the wagon.

Chloe cradled Granny in her arms, rocking back and forth. Her face shone wet in the meager light. His heart dropped to his feet when he realized the old woman was dead.

"What happened?"

"He killed her. That man I killed, he kicked her until her belly broke. I should have killed him twice, made him suffer longer." Her ragged words came from deep inside a well of pain. "She knew she was dying, dammit, and didn't say anything about it."

He crept closer, trying to determine exactly what to do. "Oh, honey, I'm sorry." The words were inadequate. He knew her pain, felt his own at the loss of the old woman. She had played such a part of him finding and falling for Chloe.

"We have to bury her proper. I'm not leaving her out here all alone." She cupped her grandmother's cheek with the gentlest touch. "Without her, I'd be nothing."

Gideon wanted to take her pain away, to erase the naked grief on her face. "We will take her to Tanger, if it's all right with you."

She nodded. "I need to get her cleaned up. Covered in your own shit ain't no way to be buried." Chloe crawled out from under the wagon, then turned to drag her grandmother's body out on the blanket.

Gideon made a move to help her, and she snarled at him. He held up his hands, knowing she had to do what she had to do. One thing Chloe had in abundance was pride, which she had in common with him. The other Devils cleared a path for her as she dragged and tugged her burden out. Her breath came in bursts as she worked, the weight of the small woman not much less than her own. Hazel and Martha jumped out of the wagon and tried to help Chloe move Granny.

"That's a helluva woman you got there, Gid," Jake said under his breath.

The men could only stand by, feeling helpless at the painful sight of the three small figures and the tragedy that had once again reared its ugly head and bitten the Ruskin family.

Gideon rose and gathered the canteens. He watched as Chloe and the girls struggled with their burden, knowing they grieved with each step they took. They stopped near the fire where Chloe could see what she was doing. He emptied the canteens into the pot they had purchased and brought it to her along with his neckerchief. Nate appeared with a clean blanket.

Like a silent, tragic dance, the men stood while Chloe cleaned her grandmother, the girls sitting by her side. She then wrapped her frail, lifeless body in the blanket. It was a requiem for Granny.

Chloe was numb. She drove the team without thinking about what she was doing, unable to let herself think because then she would feel. Gideon told her they were less than a day's ride from Tanger, and the minutes passed by with excruciating slowness. She couldn't focus on anything but the loss of her grandmother and the anchor she had relied on all her life.

Gideon rode in the back of the wagon with the girls. He'd wanted to ride with her, but she refused to let him re-injure himself. Besides, she needed time alone, and given that she was traveling with seven other people, it was the best she could get.

She had promised Granny she would hold on to the happiness in front of her, but right about then, it was too hard to think about it.

"There it is." Gideon appeared behind her, his arm outstretched, pointing in the distance.

The sun had just set behind them, washing the town in a bluish gray color. It looked peaceful and normal, like a town should. No big graveyards or burned-out hulking buildings or salted fields. A welcoming sight, enough that her cloud of misery began to lift.

"Where do you live?"

"Above the restaurant. It's that yellow building there." He gestured to a two-story building that was newer looking than other ones in town.

She didn't know if she was excited or not, but the girls sure were. They whooped and jumped up and down until Gideon told them to stop before they fell out of the wagon. They listened to him right away, and Chloe remembered just how lucky she was to have him.

Within half an hour, they were driving down the main street in Tanger. People stopped and waved at them as they passed. Many folks called the men by name, and all were friendly. Even some fancy woman stepped out of a saloon marked Aphrodite's and shouted to them.

"About time you fellas came back. It was getting mighty boring without the Blackwoods." She winked at Zeke, and to Chloe's surprise, she thought she saw him blush.

"Lucy, you leave him alone now." A blonde and very pregnant woman stood outside the jail, spearing the fancy woman with a glare.

"I ain't touched him, Naomi. He's all yours." With a flounce of her hair—in a shade of red that wasn't God-given—the woman disappeared back into the saloon.

Zeke looked at Gideon, then at Naomi.

"Go ahead. We can do what needs to be done." Gideon glanced at Chloe. "It's his wife."

"I figured."

There was a squeal behind them as Zeke reached his wife. The sound was one of joy, and it echoed through Chloe's heart. What kind of town was this? People were friendly and happy—it defied reason for her. She'd never lived in such a place. Maybe she had died right along with Granny and this was heaven.

She stopped the wagon in front of Elmer's Restaurant and set the brake. She'd journeyed from one end of life to another and was so exhausted she didn't think she could get out of the wagon by herself. Gideon solved that problem by plucking her from the seat and setting her on the sidewalk in front of the restaurant. He kissed her forehead and went back for the girls.

"If you don't mind, Chloe, Nate and I can take your grandmother to the undertaker." Jake had climbed into the wagon seat. "We can bring back whatever you need for tonight from the wagon."

Chloe nodded her thanks and held back the tears that threatened. There would be plenty of time for more grieving when they buried her grandmother. Now Chloe needed to take care of herself.

"Much obliged, Jake. Talk to Gabby and see if the girls can stay at the mill with you. I know they'd love to visit with Rebecca." Gideon squatted down to talk to the girls. "After supper, Uncle Jake is gonna bring you over to meet his little girl. She's only a baby, but I know you will have fun with her."

The girls nodded, their blonde braids bouncing with the movement.

Just like that, Gideon and his friends had taken care of everything. For once, Chloe was glad to have someone else make decisions for her.

There were a few diners in the restaurant who said hello to the Blackwoods as the group sat at a table by the window. Lee disappeared into the kitchen and reappeared only a few minutes later with two others carrying plates piled high with meat, mashed potatoes and greens. They all dug in as if they hadn't eaten in years.

Chloe focused on the food and filling her belly, rather than on anything else. A feeling of peace crept its way into her heart, and by the time she had finished eating, she felt better in body and spirit.

Gideon spoke softly to the girls, and they went into the kitchen with Lee, leaving Chloe alone with her future husband. He took her hand and kissed the back, his lips warm against her skin. She closed her eyes at the sensation. It was one she could definitely get used to.

"Are you okay?"

She managed to nod. "Sometimes I still feel the wagon moving under me. I spent months on that seat."

He squeezed her hands. "Your journey is over now. You're home."

Chloe stared into his beautiful eyes and saw the love there shining just for her. Granny was right. Chloe had everything she needed or wanted right here. She was home.

The sun was barely above the horizon when the Blackwoods gathered in the cemetery. Granny's burial was well attended since the Devils numbered fourteen with wives and children included. Gideon was proud of Chloe's strength, how she said goodbye to her Granny and took care of the girls during the ceremony. Reverend Conley presided, speaking prayers over her and arranging for the grave and coffin.

"Miss Ruskin, do you want to say a few words?"

Chloe nodded and stepped forward. She wore a dark blue dress Lee's wife, Genny, had given her. They were about the same size, and Genny was a genius with a sewing needle. Gideon didn't tell Chloe that Genny had made it the night before especially for her. She would have refused it, given her healthy dose of pride. She looked beautiful in it, and he'd need to tell her that later.

"Granny was a good woman. She didn't always make good choices, but sometimes they were the best kind." She met Gideon's gaze, and he saw his future staring back at him. "I know she'd love this town and you folks too. I'm sorry you didn't all know her like I did. The sun ain't shining as bright today now that she's gone, but I know she's looking down on me, telling me to hurry it up."

A few people chuckled, and Chloe smiled shakily. "Thank you folks for everything you done." She picked up a handful of dirt and threw it on the pine coffin. "I love you, Granny."

The girls mimicked what she had done, their little hands tossing a tiny bit of dirt. Both of them added a scrap of blue ribbon in too. His throat got tight at the memory of the last two weeks and how his life had completely changed. For the good, this time.

He pulled Chloe under his arm, and the girls each grabbed one of his legs. However awkward it was to walk, they made their way back to the restaurant for breakfast. They had closed it that morning to give the Ruskins a chance to grieve and, he hoped, a chance to get to know their new family.

Reverend Conley was only a few minutes behind him. "Gideon."

He turned to see Cindy Cooley hovering behind the young minister and wondered exactly what was happening. "Go on inside, girls, I'll be right there." He kissed Chloe quickly. "Love you."

She frowned at him but took the girls in to eat.

Gideon turned back to the couple. "Thank you for everything, Greg." He handed him a twenty-dollar gold piece. "This should be enough to cover all expenses."

"Ridiculous, of course. I won't take it." Greg tried to hand it back, but Gideon held up his hands.

"Think of it as a donation to the church, then." He grinned as the brown-haired younger man tucked it in his pocket.

"Thank you for your generosity, then." Greg looked behind him and pulled Cindy forward. "I just wanted you to be the first to know that Cindy has agreed to marry me."

Gideon should have been surprised, but he wasn't. Cindy had hidden in the mill for a couple years, since the Devils rescued her from the men who had kidnapped and done unspeakable harm to her. She was part-owner in the restaurant her grandfather had started but hadn't stepped foot in it since Gideon and Lee took on running it.

"Congratulations. That's wonderful! I have news of my own too. I'm marrying Chloe Ruskin." Gideon's smile was so wide it made his cheeks hurt. The pleasure of saying it out loud was just too much to contain though.

"I never expected it to happen so quickly, but you Blackwoods find a mate and that's that." Greg grinned back at him.

"Cindy, I'm happy for you." Gideon held out his hand. To his surprise, Cindy took it, and he pulled her into a brief hug. "You deserve to be happy."

She stepped back and offered him a small smile.

"Couldn't be better news." Gideon handed her back to Greg. "Will you join us for breakfast?"

Cindy looked in the window and hesitantly nodded. Greg took her hand with a wide grin. "Wouldn't miss it."

When Gideon entered the restaurant, he saw his family, his friends, and then he glanced at Chloe. Her curls stuck up every which way, her eyes were puffy and her face tear-stained. She'd never looked more beautiful to him. As he took her into his arms, the simple joy of hugging the woman he loved made his eyes prick with tears.

Chloe stepped into Gideon's room, the twilight making everything a shadowed gray. She'd slept there the night before, wrapped in his arms, but had been too tired to notice her surroundings. He was downstairs cleaning the restaurant. Most men didn't clean, so it was definitely something she could get used to. Hazel and Martha had gone home with Jake and his beautiful tall wife Gabriella. The twins had taken a shine to the baby, Rebecca, and Chloe knew they were in good hands.

Chloe looked around the room, snooping a bit. Gideon didn't have much in terms of personal things. There were a few books, his pistols and rifle, some clothes hanging on hooks. Nothing else marked this room as his, almost as if he was simply staying there instead of living there.

"Pretty sparse, isn't it?" His voice startled her, and she yelped. "Sorry, honey. I didn't mean to scare you."

"You didn't scare me, just gave me a start." She pressed her hand to her heart. "You are the quietest big man I ever met."

He shrugged. "Habit."

She knew he was talking about the war, but she didn't want to go any further in that conversation. Today was a day about moving on, not staying in the past. Chloe started unbuttoning the pretty blue dress Genny had given her. Lee's wife was the most similar in size and background as Chloe, and she liked her quite a bit. In fact, she liked all of the Blackwoods and knew she was lucky to have found them.

"Before I got here, I thought family was people you shared blood with. Your kin." She shook her head. "I was dead wrong. Family is people who love you and who you love, no matter what blood they have. You're my family now because I love you." She swallowed the lump that had formed.

"I love you too, honey." He started unbuttoning his own shirt while his gaze followed her hands as she continued to undress.

Chloe felt a surge of pure love for this man. She smiled at him. "That reverend better marry us soon, since we're committing a sin." She stepped toward him and put his hands on her aching bare breasts. "I don't plan on waiting till you say I do to be naked with you again."

"Thank God." He dropped to his knees and took a breast into his mouth.

Chloe gasped at the sensation, holding his head steady as he pleasured her. His tongue lapped at the nipple, and then he nibbled at it. She groaned as her pussy started pulsing with each swipe and nip. He knew exactly what she liked.

He scooped her into his arms and laid her on the bed more gently than she thought possible. "You are so beautiful it makes my heart pound to look at you."

Chloe felt beautiful. In his eyes, she saw herself as someone who was loved and cherished.

"Come here, then, and show me."

He shucked the rest of his clothes and climbed into bed, covering her with his warmth, his hardness. She spread her legs, and he slid into her welcoming core, wet with need for him. They had been together numerous times, but this was different. Every bit of her body rose to meet his. Each thrust was like the note of a song, and she was the instrument he played. They spoke to each other with their bodies, pledging themselves, declaring their love without saying a word.

This was a gentle lovemaking, one she rejoiced in as the new person she had become. Chloe's mouth found his as they both reached their peak. Pleasure washed through her, stealing her breath, stopping her heart. Gideon had breathed life back into her heart and soul.

He tucked her under his arm and pulled a quilt up over them. As Chloe drifted off, safe in the arms of the man she loved, she knew she had found where she belonged. In the arms of a Devil named Gideon.

About the Author

Beth has never been able to escape her imagination and it led her to the craft of writing romance novels. She's passionate about purple, books, and her family (not to mention long cruises). She works full-time and writes romance novels evening, weekends, early mornings and whenever there is a break in the madness.

She is compassionate, funny, a bit reserved at times, tenacious and a little quirky. Her cowboys and western romances speak of a bygone era, bringing her readers to an age where men were honest, hard and honkin' built.

For a change of pace, she also dives into some smokin' hot contemporaries, bringing you heat, romance and snappy dialogue.

To learn more about Beth Williamson, please visit www.bethwilliamson.com or send an email to Beth at beth@bethwilliamson.com.

Life is cheap. So is death.

Maiden Lane
© 2011 Lynne Connolly
Richard and Rose, Book 7

With Rose expecting again, it should be a joyous time for her and Richard. Yet old enemies and new come out of the woodwork, seemingly intent on using whatever means possible to destroy their happiness. Not only is the legitimacy of their marriage called into question, a young man steps forward claiming to be a by-blow of Richard's dark, wild past.

Closer to defeat than he has ever been, Richard musters all his friends and allies to defend against this attack on his own ground. However, no amount of incandescent lovemaking and tender care seems to keep Rose out of harm's way.

Then a mutilated body turns up on their doorstep—and all fingers point at Richard. Rose has no choice but to emerge from his near-smothering concern to do what she must to save the love of her life. Even if she must appear to work against him.

As she lays her heart on the line, Richard fights to keep the violence that marks his past from claiming her life. For if he loses Rose, with her will go his humanity.

Warning: Rose gets her mad on, and Richard gets turned on. Contains married love, married sex and married fooling about. And pink coats with lace ruffles. And swords. And wicked goings-on.

Available now in ebook and print from Samhain Publishing.

Romance

HORROR

www.samhainpublishing.com

CPSIA information can be obtained at www.ICGtesting.com
Printed in the USA
BVOW011249190212

283266BV00001B/37/P